C46379788L

10658730

}

18

2019

U19

JT496:

1 6 DEC 2019

-3 JAN 2020

SPECIAL MESSAGE TO READERS

THE ULVERSCROFT FOUNDATION
(registered UK charity number 264873)

was established in 1972 to provide funds for research, diagnosis and treatment of eye diseases. Examples of major projects funded by the Ulverscroft Foundation are:-

- The Children's Eye Unit at Moorfields Eye Hospital, London
- The Ulverscroft Children's Eye Unit at Great Ormond Street Hospital for Sick Children
- Funding research into eye diseases and treatment at the Department of Ophthalmology, University of Leicester
- The Ulverscroft Vision Research Group, Institute of Child Health
- Twin operating theatres at the Western Ophthalmic Hospital, London
- The Chair of Ophthalmology at the Royal Australian College of Ophthalmologists

You can help further the work of the Foundation by making a donation or leaving a legacy. Every contribution is gratefully received. If you would like to help support the Foundation or require further information, please contact:

THE ULVERSCROFT FOUNDATION
The Green, Bradgate Road, Anstey
Leicester LE7 7FU, England
Tel: (0116) 236 4325

website: www.foundation.ulverscroft.com

First published in Great Britain in 2015

First Linford Edition
published 2016

Copyright © 2015 by Miranda Barnes
All rights reserved

A catalogue record for this book is available
from the British Library.

ISBN 978–1–4448–2910–5

Published by
F. A. Thorpe (Publishing)
Anstey, Leicestershire

Set by Words & Graphics Ltd.
Anstey, Leicestershire
Printed and bound in Great Britain by
T. J. International Ltd., Padstow, Cornwall

This book is printed on acid-free paper

SOUTH LANARKSHIRE LIBRARIES

MIRANDA BARNES

---◆---

ORKNEY
MYSTERY

Complete and Unabridged

LINFORD
Leicester

Books by Miranda Barnes
in the Linford Romance Library:

DAYS LIKE THESE
A NEW BEGINNING
IT WAS ALWAYS YOU
THE HOUSE ON THE HILL
MYSTERY AT CASA LARGO

ORKNEY MYSTERY

When Emma Mason inherits a house on Orkney from her Great-aunt Freda, she is mystified — she knows nothing about Freda, and her parents are of little help. The only thing for it is to visit Orkney herself. On the ferry, she meets Gregor McEwan, a wildlife photographer and passionate Orcadian. Together they begin to piece together Freda's story, whilst becoming increasingly attracted to each other — though there are serious obstacles in their way: Gregor is struggling with a past tragedy, and Emma's life is firmly rooted in Tyneside . . .

1

She had heard that the Pentland Firth was a lot rougher than the English Channel. That was proved to be true as soon as the ship left the harbour at Scrabster, just outside Thurso, and ventured out into the wild seas beyond the north coast of mainland Scotland. Orkney, invisible in the mist and the spray, seemed impossibly far away as the ship began to lurch and sway alarmingly.

Well, they did warn me, Emma thought with a grimace, as her stomach experienced turmoil. *They did tell me not to bother coming here. There was no need for it, Anna and Kim both said. And it was true. There wasn't. I didn't have to come. I could have gone on holiday with them. I'm sure Aunt Freda wouldn't have minded, bless her. But did I listen? Oh, no. Not me! I had*

to do it my way, as usual.

Gripping tables and head rests desperately for support, she lurched across the lounge and collapsed thankfully into a vacant seat. *I could have been on a Greek island with my friends,* she reminded herself, *enjoying warm spring sunshine and a flat, tranquil sea. Dancing in a taverna on the beach. Sipping wine at the day's end. Or just coming out of the sea, to let the sun dry my beautifully tanned skin. My hair curly with sun and sea,* she added even more fancifully. *Instead, here I am. Having to put up with this! Serves me right for being so stubborn and contrary. Oh, why didn't I listen? I'm going to be sick. Any minute now, I'm going to . . . Oh, I hate this ship! I hate Orkney, as well, even though I haven't seen it yet.*

An elderly woman sitting in a neighbouring seat leant forward and smiled sympathetically. 'Is the ship's movement getting to you?' she asked.

'Just a little,' Emma admitted with

another grimace. 'I'm not a good sailor. I should have flown.'

'Oh, no! This is by far the best way to travel to the islands. Just try to relax, dear. Stop obsessing about your poor stomach. Don't even think about it!'

'I'm trying very hard already. Really I am.'

'And doing very well, if you don't mind my saying so. Och, away! You'll be fine once you find your sea legs.'

Such confidence, Emma thought miserably. *I wish I had some of it. As for my sea legs, I don't believe I have any, and never have had.*

'At least we'll be across the firth before the storm arrives,' the woman added. 'I doubt there'll be any more sailings after this one for a day or so.'

'A storm?' Emma shuddered. 'Don't tell me there's going to be a storm as well!'

The woman nodded. 'So they say, the weather forecasters. And they're usually right about what they say for the Northern Isles.'

That shut Emma up, as again she considered how she hadn't really needed to be here. A storm? Wasn't what they had right now enough?

'Is this your first visit to Orkney?' the woman asked.

Emma nodded. Her smile froze for a moment as the ship dropped sickeningly. Then she rallied as it rose back up again, and she added bravely, 'I've been across the channel a few times, though. So I hoped I would be all right.'

'Oh? Which channel will that be, dear?'

'The English . . . ' Emma stopped when she saw the woman was smiling mischievously. 'Mind you,' she added with a chuckle, 'each time the ferry left Dover I decided I would fly the next time.'

Her companion laughed. 'I've been from Dover to Calais myself. But the English Channel is not a bit like the Pentland Firth. There's nothing to compare with genuine Scottish weather and seas, I can assure you — unless it's

4

what they have around the Faroes and Iceland!'

'And Greenland, perhaps?' Emma said with a smile, warming to this friendly soul who had such a mischievous twinkle in her eye.

'Indeed. Greenland, too. I often feel so sorry for the poor fishermen that go off up that way, especially in the depths of winter. But they're hardy people. They manage, just as islanders always have done.'

'I was going to go to a Greek island with my friends,' Emma said ruefully, 'but something came up, and I changed my mind. I hope I've not made a mistake.'

'Och, no! Of course you haven't. You'll not regret coming to Orkney, storm or no storm. I've lived here all my life, and I can tell you now there's no place like it.'

Emma wasn't sure that was a recommendation worth anything more than a diplomatic smile. Already, she regretted coming. She wouldn't have been on this ship if she'd gone to Greece instead.

'Now, if you'll excuse me,' the woman added, 'I must be away to look in the peedie shop they have onboard. I have grandbairns who will be expecting me to bring them something from my trip to Scotland, and I didn't have time to look around for anything in Thurso.'

The *peedie* shop? Emma wondered. What on earth was that?

Later, when she was more used to the movement of the ferry, and her stomach was no longer sending out shrieks of discomfort, and even outrage, Emma wondered if the woman was right to be so sure she would enjoy Orkney. She certainly hoped so. This trip was taking a big chunk out of her annual holiday allowance. She didn't want it to be wasted.

Not that it would be wasted, of course, even if she hated the place. After all, she reminded herself, she wasn't really coming for a holiday, not as such. She was coming to see the house, and to decide what to do with it. That was the only reason she was here at all really, aboard this dreadful ship. After all, if someone was so kind as to leave you a house in their will, the very least you could do — after saying, or thinking, thank-you, of course — was to look at it before you sold it. She owed Aunt Freda that much, even if she couldn't recall ever actually meeting the dear old lady.

2

A little later still, Emma summoned up enough courage to venture out onto the viewing deck at the rear of the ship. By then her stomach was becoming a little more accustomed to the wild lurching and swaying, the upward thrusts and the sickening drops. Disaster still threatened, and was still very possible, though it wasn't quite so imminent. She didn't feel she was about to be violently sick at any minute. Her hope was that a breath of fresh air might help settle things down even more.

Far from a breath of fresh air, she got a full blast of it in her face when she negotiated the air lock between two doors and stepped outside. The wind was ferocious. She ducked her head and closed her eyes for a moment to deal with the shock.

'Steady!'

8

A hand gripped her by the elbow. She opened her eyes and tried to smile at the man supporting her. He looked concerned.

'This wind!' she said apologetically. 'It took my breath away for a moment.'

'I saw that. You OK now?'

'Yes, thank you.'

'There's a bit of shelter on this side,' the man said, steering her away from the doorway and into an alcove shielded from the wind.

She nodded her thanks and straightened up to look around. 'Oh! Are we there already?' she asked, seeing a dark line of cliffs through the mist.

The man shook his head. 'Not yet. It'll be another hour before we reach Stromness. That's the island of Hoy coming up there, on the starboard side.'

Emma stared out at the approaching island with apprehension. All she could see was a long, towering wall of rock. Waves were breaking at the foot of it in a white fury and sending spray high up the cliff face.

'Hoy?' she said, thinking the name sounded vaguely familiar.

'Indeed,' the man said. 'And if you look closely, you can pick out the Old Man of Hoy, just over there.'

She peered through the mist and gloom. At first she couldn't see what he meant.

'The rock pinnacle. See it?'

'Oh, yes! Now I can — I think.'

A slender tower of rock stood in front of the high cliff face, separated from it by the raging sea.

'They call that pinnacle the Old Man of Hoy?'

'They do indeed.'

'Oh, yes! Hasn't someone climbed it?' she asked with a puzzled frown. 'I seem to remember noticing something in the paper about it a while back, but surely that would be impossible?'

'It's been climbed a few times, actually. Back in the sixties, a TV crew broadcast a live programme of a team led by Joe Brown climbing it over a three-day period. But last year Chris

Bonington, the man who made the very first ascent, came back to climb it again to mark his eightieth birthday.'

'Goodness!' Emma was astonished. It seemed an utterly impossible feat. How could anyone at all climb it, let alone someone that age?

'And that's the Old Man of Hoy for you!' her companion said with a grin. 'This your first visit to the islands?' he added, changing tack.

She nodded, and then lurched sideways as the ship began to turn. The man grabbed her by the elbow again and said, 'You'll find your sea legs eventually.'

'If I live that long,' she said grimly, thinking it was the second time she had been told that.

He laughed.

'But if it happens, it can't come soon enough,' Emma assured him, managing a token smile. 'At least I feel better out here on deck. My stomach has stopped trying to leave me.'

'I always feel better outside,' he said,

nodding in agreement. 'Mother likes to be inside, out of the wind, but I prefer it out here. Where is she, by the way?'

'Who?' Emma asked, puzzled.

'Mother. I saw you talking to her in the lounge.'

'Oh, that nice old lady? I didn't realise. She said she was off to the peedie shop, whatever that is.'

He laughed. 'Little shop, she meant.'

'Ah!'

'You'll no doubt hear a few more new words while you're up here in Orkney. Holiday, is it?'

'Sort of. I'm just visiting, at least. How about you?'

'Oh, I'm a native, like Mother. Our family has always lived here. Kirkwall, the capital, is where we live. Where are you headed, by the way?'

'A place called Birsay, on the mainland. Do you know it?'

He nodded. 'My brother lives there.'

'What's it like?'

'Remote. Good for birds, though,' he said, grinning. 'Especially at this time of year — late winter, early spring.'

'Birds?' she said with a shudder. 'What about people? Me, for instance? What's it like for us?'

'Well, maybe you would like it better in summer. It's an area rather than a place, by the way. There is a village, but normally we're talking about the locality when we say Birsay. Anyway, I hope you enjoy it.'

'Is it windy there?'

He looked at her sternly and said, 'Oh, yes! Wind is something we do very well on Orkney. Get used to it!'

★   ★   ★

Emma stayed on deck most of the rest of the way, talking to the man who had helped her. He said his name was Gregor McEwan. He was a freelance wildlife cameraman and photographer based on his home island.

'Orkney's a good place for you to work, I take it?' Emma said.

'Perfect. Occasionally I get the urge

to go off to see elephants and tigers, but the birds and the seals always bring me back home before long. Here, at least, I'm a real expert.'

'How wonderful,' she said. 'It sounds a lovely way to make a living.'

'It's what I always wanted to do. Simple as that. How about you?'

'Me? Oh, I don't do anything very special. I just work for an insurance company in Newcastle — a back-office job.'

'Like it?'

She shrugged. 'Well . . . It's a good job, but I don't have a sense of vocation about it. Nothing like that. But I've been there since not long after I left school. So, yes, I suppose I must like it.'

'Do you live in the city?'

'Fenham, on the outskirts. Do you know Tyneside?'

He nodded. 'I've been there a few times, passing through.'

'But you prefer here?'

He just grinned. Then he turned to point at some land on the other side of

14

the ship. 'That's the tip of the Mainland. We'll be in Stromness in a few minutes.'

'Is it a big town?'

'It is by Orkney standards, but not by yours. It's the second-biggest town on the islands, after Kirkwall, the capital. It used to be busier and a lot more important than it is now, though. Whalers would sail from here, and the Hudson's Bay Company ships.'

'Really? I've heard of them. They were important for the fur trade and the exploration of Canada, I seem to recall?'

'That's right. They were.'

'So what was the company doing here?'

'Oh, trading and outfitting. Repairing the ships. A lot of the company's employees came from Orkney. The building where they used to recruit the men is still here, in Stromness. It's a museum now. Then there's the gun, out along the foreshore, which they used to fire whenever a company ship came into port.' He paused, grinned and added, 'I haven't even mentioned Dr John Rae yet. He was from Stromness.'

'Who?'

'He was the man they asked to go looking for the Franklin expedition.'

'I'm sorry to be so ignorant, but what was that?'

'Franklin's two ships were lost in the search for the north-west passage in about 1850. What happened to them was a mystery until very recently, when one of the wrecked ships was found at last.'

'So there's a lot of history here.'

'Oh, yes! Indeed there is. And we Orcadians are very liable to start telling you about it at the slightest invitation.' He sighed and added, 'Now I'd better go and find Mother. She'll be getting worried I've fallen overboard. Do you need a lift when we get ashore, by the way?'

'No, thanks. I have my own car.'

'Right. Well, it was nice meeting you, Emma. I hope you have an enjoyable stay — and that you'll want to come back again!'

He shook her hand and left. She rather regretted his going. He was a very attractive and charming young man, she thought wistfully. She had enjoyed his company, and had liked his mother as well. So, seemingly, had her poor stomach. She no longer felt sick at all. What a pity she couldn't travel further with the two of them.

By now, the ship had reached the edge of the town. Emma stayed where she was and watched as more and more of it came into view: little cottages on the gentle hillside at first, then a harbour with fishermen's cottages lining it, each seemingly with its own slipway for launching a fishing boat. Commercial buildings came next, and all the paraphernalia of a fishing town. Bigger boats. Landing stages. Docks within the harbour. Houses spreading up the hillside behind the town.

At last, the ferry terminal arrived. The ship slowed and turned. She was here. Stromness. Orkney. When the captain's voice came over the loud-speaker system to announce their arrival, she left the rail and began to make her way down to the car deck.

3

Heavy rain was slanting in on a cold, gusting wind by the time Emma was able to drive her car off the ferry. It definitely wasn't a good time to be sightseeing in Stromness. She pulled into a car park beside the harbour and studied her map for a few minutes, refreshing her memory. Then she got going. The sooner she reached Birsay, the better, she decided. In fact, the sooner she could have a hot bath and climb into bed, the better!

Holiday? Huh! Today had been an ordeal rather than a pleasure, and it wasn't over yet.

The rain crashed against the windscreen as she headed out of town. She grimaced, kept her speed down and concentrated on what she could see of the road ahead. About fifteen or twenty miles to go, she estimated. In these conditions, she would be lucky to get there by tomorrow morning.

What a choice she'd made! Right about now, her friends would be enjoying themselves on a Greek island. Crete, Rhodes, Kos? She couldn't even remember which one they had finally chosen. As she wasn't going, she had lost interest. She hadn't wanted to be weighed down with all the redundant detail. It was just Greece, a Greek island, to her. Whichever one it was, though, it would be sunny and hot — and definitely not windy and rainy! In comparison, these islands that she'd got stuck with were absolute rubbish. There was no other word for them. Envy? Not a bit of it!

What on earth could have made Aunt Freda choose to live here most of her life? She must have been dotty. Probably the wind had made her like that. Just listen to it!

Emma screwed her face up as the scream of the wind reached a new pitch. She even pulled over to the side of the road for a minute or two, wondering if she wanted to go any further. Then she started off again. She didn't really have a choice. She wasn't going to let the weather defeat her. Besides, she had a reservation at the B&B. The people there would be expecting her. She couldn't let them down.

When she arrived, she went directly to Davar, the guesthouse she had booked online. Her late aunt's home, Broch House, wasn't far away according to the map, but she decided seeing it could wait until the storm had passed over. At the moment she just wanted to get inside somewhere warm and dry.

'Hello!' The young woman who opened the door had a big welcoming smile on her face, as well as a baby on her hip. 'You must be Emma?'

'That's right,' she said, smiling back. 'Emma Mason. And you're Jenny?'

'Yes, I am. My husband, Neil, is around somewhere. You'll meet him soon enough. Come in, come in! I'll

21

take your wet coat and hang it up to dry. How was your journey?'

'Fine — until the storm arrived,' Emma said with a grimace.

'Och, that's Orkney for you! Just a bit of wind and rain. It'll be different again tomorrow. You'll see.'

'I certainly hope so.'

★ ★ ★

Sure enough, by the next morning the storm had abated. The rain had stopped and the ferocious wind had become a gentle breeze. There was even a hint of sunshine behind the thin cloud cover. After breakfast Emma set off to see her inheritance, leaving the car behind. Broch House wasn't far away. A mere ten minute walk, according to her hosts.

Even with their instructions, the approach wasn't obvious, however. She was glad to encounter a friendly elderly man standing at his garden gate, watching her approach along the lane. 'Can I help you?' he asked when she was close.

She didn't really need help, but it was hard to refuse the offer of it. 'Broch House?' she asked with a smile. 'Do you know where it is?'

'Broch House, is it, you're wanting, eh? Old Miss Nicholson's place. It's been closed and empty a wee while now, though.'

'Yes, I know. I'm Miss Nicholson's niece.'

'Och, you know all about it, then,' he said with a nod and a smile. 'Just carry on down the road a little way. You can't miss it. It's the house with the two trees in front.' He pointed the way ahead and added, 'The first one in the village, or the last, depending which way you're coming from.'

'Thank you!' Emma smiled and added, 'Has the storm given up, do you think?'

'For now, perhaps.' He looked up at the sky and added, 'But for how long, though?'

'Indeed!'

She gave him a cheery wave and went

on her way, wondering if all the natives were as friendly as him.

As she neared Broch House, she could see that it was quite a large two-storey house. Not a cosy little cottage at all, she thought with surprise.

She opened the garden gate and stood just inside for a few moments, running her eye over things. Surrounded by a hedge that had got out of control, and with two big sycamore trees either side of the gate, the garden had obviously been fairly well-tended in the past. Now, though, it had become rather wild. She could see brambles competing with roses, and dandelions threatening to take over the lawn. The struggle must have become too much for Aunt Freda, which wasn't really surprising. Her aunt had been a good age.

The house itself was a very plain-looking, grey, pebble-dashed building. It was double-fronted, with an attractive little porch on stone pillars sheltering the front door. The small sash windows, upstairs and down, all looked as though they wanted a good clean, but they seemed in good repair.

In fact, Emma's first impression, admittedly from the outside, was that the house as a whole was in pretty good condition. Aunt Freda must have been on top of things until almost the very end. Such a big house, too. She really had done very well.

Emma walked down the path leading to the front door and fumbled out the keys she had received from the solicitor back in Newcastle. Then she paused for a moment and took a deep breath, wondering with some trepidation what awaited her on the other side of the door.

The first thing she noticed inside was the smell. She wrinkled her nose and grimaced. Damp! The house smelled damp and unoccupied, which was exactly what it was. She wondered how long it had been like that. A few months, certainly. But so far no one had been able to tell her exactly when her aunt had passed away. She steeled herself to begin her inspection.

Two big reception rooms opened off the hall. Both were fully furnished with ancient, if comfortable-looking, items that might have been acquired from a museum dedicated to the 1940s. Sofas with tassels, sideboards, and wing-backed chairs. Tall oak bookshelves brimming with books, and a pine dresser displaying an ornate porcelain tea service.

Emma smiled as she contemplated the first of the rooms, and smiled even more broadly when she looked into the second. How clever! One was clearly the morning room, receiving full sun — as it did now — through big windows overlooking a lawn. The other was darker, cosier — more of an evening room — with only one small window. She couldn't believe the second room ever got any sun at all, but she could imagine it being a comfortable place to retreat to of a winter's evening.

The well-worn chair and stack of logs

by the open fireplace told her where Aunt Freda had liked to be by that time of day. She crossed the room to examine the book shelves on the far side. Her aunt had obviously been a reader, she thought, impressed. There were some wonderful books here, fiction and non-fiction, and quite a few modern publications as well as many classics.

She glanced around. No television. She smiled again. Of course not! No time for that, when you had all these lovely books to read. There was even an ancient chaise longue, well-worn, to allow you to do that in some comfort. And if it was cool, the wing-backed chair close to the fireplace looked just the place to be.

The house was centrally heated, though; the old lady had seen to that. There were big radiators on two walls in this room, the evening room. She had noticed that the other room, the morning room, also had radiators, but they would scarcely be needed when the sun was shining.

She moved on, and found the kitchen. That raised another smile. It was a big room, with a lovely old farmhouse table in the centre. Definitely a traditional kitchen. Not a microwave in sight. There was an Aga cooker on one side. For times when speed was needed, there was also an electric cooker, with separate oven and hob, not far away. The Aga would be lovely in winter, but too much perhaps in summer — if they ever got summer here, she added with a shiver, the general damp coolness of the house getting to her suddenly.

Surprisingly, there were six bedrooms upstairs, three doubles and three singles. Two of the bedrooms were fully furnished, one of them obviously Aunt Freda's, and the other perhaps a visitor's room. The remaining rooms had beds, but otherwise only essential furniture.

There was also a well-fitted and large bathroom with a big free-standing bath and a separate shower cubicle. It looked to be the most modern room in the house. And why not? Emma thought with approval. Some things mattered more than others, and this was one of them.

All in all, she concluded, the house was surprisingly big — much too big for a single, elderly lady. Still, she thought, Aunt Freda wasn't always elderly, and perhaps she wasn't always single either. Really, and sadly, she knew next to nothing about her.

Another conclusion was that despite its plain exterior, the house was rather a pleasant old place. Parts of it were even quite cosy. The kitchen and evening room, for example. And the bathroom. Yet it was so big that Aunt Freda could only have lived in part of it, certainly in recent times. How strange. Why hadn't she moved into something smaller?

Overall, though, it wasn't bad, she decided with relief. It needed updating, as the estate agents would say, but it was a substantial house in good repair. No doubt Aunt Freda had seen no need at all to update it. It had probably suited her just fine exactly as it was. No mystery about that at all, really.

4

As Emma was leaving, closing the gate carefully after her, a man walking along the road came up to speak to her.

'Good morning! You must be the niece?'

She turned and smiled politely. 'Good morning. Yes, I'm Miss Nicholson's niece.'

'I heard you'd come to look at the old place.'

Now who would he have heard that from? Emma wondered. It could only have been the elderly man who had told her the way here. She hadn't spoken to anyone else. News travelled fast in these parts, seemingly.

'Do you live locally?' she asked politely.

'Aye. In the village, there. I knew your aunt quite well.'

Emma nodded. She wasn't eager to

get into a conversation about either the house or her aunt with someone she didn't know.

'The house will no doubt be going up for sale?' the man inquired.

'Oh, I don't know yet,' Emma said with another polite smile. 'I've only just got here.'

'You'll not get a lot for it,' he continued as if she hadn't spoken. 'What with the state of the economy, and how it wants such a lot doing to it, the old place.' He shook his head, as if to confirm his own thinking, and added, 'Aye, you cannot expect much for it. Prices are awful low around here, anyway. And then there's the recession. It's not worth you spending any money on doing it up, either. You'd never get your money back.'

Emma nodded and started edging away. This was a conversation she did not wish to have. She wasn't impressed by the way the man had intruded on her. The house, and her plans for it, were nothing to do with him, she almost felt inclined to say.

'But I'll be happy to talk to you when it comes to putting the old place on the market,' he added. 'I might be able to help you out, as I'm a man with a growing family myself, and I'm in need of a bigger house. Alastair McEwan, by the way. Just ask for me in the village. Everybody there knows me.'

'Thank you,' she said without a smile. 'I'll remember that.'

What a cheek! she thought as she walked away. *Remember him? I should think I will!*

* * *

The young couple who owned the guesthouse invited her to have coffee with them. She did, partly to avoid another little rain shower she saw streaming over the fields towards them.

'It rains so often here!' she said, hurrying inside.

'Ten times a day,' Jenny said with what sounded like grim satisfaction.

'Twenty!' her husband, Neil, said.

Emma laughed. 'How do you stand it?'

'Och, it's what we're used to,' Neil said. 'We've both lived here all our lives. We wouldn't know what to do with good weather.'

'You were born in Birsay?'

'No, not Birsay. We're from Kirkwall — the big capital city!'

'It is big, isn't it?' Emma said with a smile.

'Indeed it is! There must be seven thousand souls living there now.'

'Goodness! As many as that?'

He grinned at her. 'Nearly as big as your Newcastle.'

'Nearly,' she admitted, enjoying the sense of fun pervading the kitchen.

Jenny brought a plate of shortbread over to the kitchen table, to complement the coffee her husband was pouring.

'Something I've been wondering,' Emma said. 'This island, the biggest of the Orkney islands — it's called

34

Mainland, right?'

'Aye,' Neil said, eyeing her suspiciously.

'So what do Orcadians call what I think of as the mainland, over there on the other side of the Pentland Firth?'

Neil and Jenny looked at each other for a moment. Then Jenny said, 'That's Scotland, of course.'

'Of course. Silly me!' Emma laughed and added, 'You make it sound like a foreign country.'

'So it is,' Neil said, 'to a large extent. Like Shetland, Orkney looks after itself. It doesn't really matter what goes on in London, or in Edinburgh either for that matter, to us up here in the Northern Isles.'

Emma nodded. 'That's the impression I've been getting,' she admitted.

'We're more interested in what's going on in Norway, and in Iceland and Faroe,' Neil continued.

'Just you speak for yourself!' Jenny intervened. 'Kirkwall is as far as I want to go when it comes to shopping, or taking the little one to see the doctor.'

Neil laughed. 'True enough!'

'Priorities, eh?' Emma said with amusement.

'You bet!' Jenny said firmly.

Emma decided she liked her hosts very much. They had such an easy, friendly way with each other, and with her. So she took the opportunity to ask them if they had known her aunt.

'Miss Nicholson, in Broch House?' Jenny said. 'Was she your aunt? Oh, yes! Everyone around here knew her. She was a lovely old lady.'

'Everyone around here knows everyone else anyway,' Neil added, 'regardless of what they're like. It's unavoidable. More's the pity.'

'Oh, Neil! What a thing to say.' Jenny shook her head, then turned back to Emma and said earnestly, 'He just means it's a very friendly community.'

'A very nosey community as well,' Neil said with a laugh. 'We all know each other's business.'

'What about a man called Alastair

36

McEwan? Do you know him?'

'Oh, he's the worst of the lot,' Neil said. 'The man's forever poking his nose into other folks' business.'

'Neil!' Jenny remonstrated. 'You make him sound terrible, and he's not. Not really.'

'Well . . . ' Neil just shrugged.

'I met him this morning,' Emma hurried to say. 'He told me I shouldn't expect much for Aunt Freda's house when I sell it, because it's in rubbish condition and the economy's terrible anyway. He made me feel I should just give it away. Then he told me to contact him when I want to sell.'

Neil laughed. 'That's him! What a terrible man he is, trying to take advantage of you so soon.'

Jenny smiled. 'I don't really think there's any harm in him. He's just . . . '

'Nosey?' Neil suggested, provoking more laughter.

'Now *I'm* being nosey,' Emma admitted. 'I know next to nothing about my aunt, even though she left me her house when she died. I would really like to know what she was like, and what she did with herself. For one thing, Broch House, nice as it is, is such a big place for an elderly woman on her own.'

'Well, we're really not the best folk to ask,' Neil said. 'We've not been here too long ourselves. We just knew her as a pleasant neighbour, and a bit of a local celebrity.'

'She was always out and about,' Jenny added. 'Walking, I mean. She seemed to be very interested in natural things — wildlife and such. Birds, particularly.'

'And ancient monuments,' her husband contributed. 'She took a great interest in them.'

'Yes, you're right.' Jenny considered for a moment and then said, 'Everything, really. She seemed to be interested in everything.'

Emma nodded thoughtfully, thinking once again how little she knew of Aunt Freda. Next to nothing. It seemed such a pity. She would have to try to find out more while she was here. She owed her that much, at least.

5

Emma returned to Broch House the following morning. This time she explored it more thoroughly, taking her time. She wanted to get a feel for the place, and to try to understand what sort of house it had been when it was lived in by Aunt Freda.

The truth was that it was all a bit of a mystery, one that was starting to intrigue her. She just couldn't imagine how an elderly woman could have lived here all alone all those years. She dearly wanted to know how her aunt had managed it, and what she had been like. What was she doing on Orkney all those years, anyway? One of the few things Emma did know about Aunt Freda was that she hadn't been born here.

Having been told by her hosts at the guesthouse that her aunt had been such an active person had made her even more curious. Something of a local celebrity, Alastair had said. In what way? And how had Aunt Freda made her living? Considering the house she had owned, she obviously hadn't been living on benefits. She must have done something that paid well at some stage in her life.

One thing Emma was sure of: she wouldn't be putting Broch House up for sale until she knew more about it, and more about Aunt Freda. She was determined about that. But unfortunately, she didn't know anyone in the family she could ask. The obvious place to go was her own family, but that hadn't been any good when she had enquired. Her mother didn't seem to know anything, and was even less interested. All she had said was that her understanding was that Aunt Freda had lived in Scotland all her life nearly, and, sorry, but she didn't know anything else about her. Mum didn't think she had ever actually even seen her. Dad, unfortunately, knew even less than that.

Really, though, Emma reflected, it should have been down to her mum. It was nothing to do with her dad, and not much more to do with herself either. Freda was actually Mum's aunt, rather than Emma's. That was about all she had been able to establish before she left home to come here. So, really, Freda had been Emma's great-aunt, or something! She shook her head with exasperation. She always had been vague about family relationships.

Dad had just shaken his head, and said he knew nothing about the woman, and not much about Mum's family in general. All he knew was that they called this woman in Scotland 'Aunt Freda', if they ever mentioned her at all — which wasn't very often — whatever the precise relationship. He had seemed to have no interest in speculating about her either.

Mum had been horrified at the idea of Emma travelling all the way to Orkney, especially alone, just to see some old house that had been left to her by someone they had never seen. Why on earth did she want to do that? Just tell the solicitors to sell it — and be done with it! That had been her poorly considered advice.

Mum hadn't even been very curious about why Emma had been left the house in the first place. Strange things happened every day, she said. Some people won the lottery, didn't they? Why them, not somebody else? There was neither rhyme nor reason to it. The same with this house.

Emma smiled as she recollected her mother's astonishment at her proposal to visit Orkney. She had been mystified. Not that she had stood in Emma's way at all. She just hadn't been able to understand it.

'It's the least I can do, Mum,' Emma had explained. 'Apart from anything else, I want to know: why me? Why has a house been left to me? I have no idea. Do you?'

Mum had shaken her head. 'No. It's

a mystery,' she had said. 'Let me know what you find out, dear. Anyway, where is Orkney? Up north somewhere, isn't it?'

'It's part of the Northern Isles, Mum, north of Scotland. Near Shetland. I looked it up in the atlas.'

'There you are, then. It's no place for you to be going. Just make sure you take plenty of warm clothes.'

'Gloves,' Dad intervened, winking at her. 'You'll want gloves.'

'And a hat and scarf, do you think?' Emma asked, tongue in cheek.

He nodded. 'Best to be on the safe side. Fur coat, as well, if you've got one.'

'You two!' Mum said. 'You're as bad as each other. It's all very well making fun of me, but it's likely to be cold — wherever Orkney is!'

Now here Emma was, rummaging through the house as if it were a cross between a crime scene and a museum, trying to make sense of Aunt Freda's life. Try as she might, though, she was having little success. For one thing, there was a disappointing lack of personal stuff in the house. Hardly any clothes at all, and very few papers. Lots of books, though. But they didn't help much.

She spent a couple of hours going through the rooms more carefully without finding much of interest. The house was so clean and tidy; it was as if Aunt Freda had taken everything away with her. What a silly thought! Emma admonished herself. She straightened up and yawned, feeling a little dispirited. Perhaps it was time she did something else. She was getting nowhere here.

She glanced out of the window and saw that the sun was shining. In fact, it was a very bright day now. The sunlight reflecting off the shimmering wet grass, as she gazed towards the sea, made a pleasing picture. Was that an island? She peered harder into the distance. She couldn't be sure, but she rather thought it was.

Well, she thought wearily, stifling a yawn, perhaps she should get outside and do a little sightseeing while the weather was so nice. She could call in at the cafe in the village she had noticed. Have a coffee, and see if anyone there had known Aunt Freda. That would be altogether more purposeful than hanging about here like this.

But once she was in the car, she changed her mind and decided it was time to visit Kirkwall, which was about twenty miles away. The journey would allow her to see a bit more of the island, as well as satisfy her curiosity about the Orkney capital.

Everywhere looked so fresh and green as she drove in a south-easterly direction. No forest or woodland, and virtually no individual trees either. Just beautifully green fields. The land was low-lying, almost level, and she could see for miles across an endless sea of grass. She had assumed she would see lots of sheep grazing, like in Northumberland, but there were very few. Instead, there seemed to be herds of black cattle everywhere.

The landscape was dotted with what

she assumed were small farmhouses, mostly modern bungalows. Occasionally she passed a ruined stone cottage, testament to times and a way of life gone by. Big modern vehicles were parked next to many of the farmhouses: pickup trucks with double cabs, and four-wheel-drive monsters. It looked to her as if whatever farming was done here was prosperous.

Then the sea came into view, and soon afterwards the town of Kirkwall, clustered around its harbour. She parked near the harbour in the centre, where the fishing boats were gathered, and wandered up a narrow access lane to the main shopping street, curious to see what was on offer.

Not a lot, she soon decided. Little shops selling ordinary, everyday things. Nothing special at all. But, then, you had to be realistic. Despite being Orkney's capital, it was a small town, about the size of Alnwick, and by the looks of it one without a lot of money. Either that, or one without much taste for extravagant expenditure on things that were not really needed.

Still, there were a couple of interesting craft shops, and she spent a few minutes in a very good bookshop that stocked an incredible number of books about Orkney. The islands seemed to be much-written about by poets, travellers, historians, and wildlife experts. Finally, at the end of the street stood a magnificent ancient church built of a deep red sandstone that was almost the colour of blood: St Magnus Cathedral.

And that seemed to be that. She had done the main street. She paused for a moment, feeling a little flat, wondering what to do next. Coffee, she decided. She had seen a very modern-looking Italian-style coffee shop not far away. She would give that a try.

★　★　★

It was as she was coming out of the coffee shop that she bumped into Gregor, the friendly young man she had met on the ferry.

'Hello again!' he said, smiling broadly. 'Have you come to see the sights? Grown tired of Birsay already?'

She laughed. 'Gregor! Fancy meeting you again.'

'Och, it's a small world, Orkney. So how are you getting on?'

'Very well, thank you. But I'd looked around the house enough for the time being, so I decided to do a little exploring.'

'House? What house?'

'Oh, didn't I tell you why I'm here?' she said, realising why he looked so puzzled. 'I have a house to sell. That's why I came to Orkney.'

'Really?' Gregor looked surprised.

'Is your brother called Alastair, by the way?'

'He is. Have you met him?'

She nodded. 'I think so. A big man who looks a bit like you, and has the same surname. Alastair McEwan?'

'That's him! Was he rude? He usually is.'

'Well . . . After he finished telling me how rubbishy the house is, he seemed to be offering to buy it.'

'Good old Ally!' Gregor said, shaking his head in sorrow. 'He's a terrible man for a bargain.'

'That's what I thought at the time. I didn't appreciate his bargaining technique, though, and I very nearly told him so.'

'I hope you don't hold me responsible?' Gregor said anxiously.

She laughed. 'Not at all! I was just surprised, that's all. He's not much like you, is he?'

'So folks say. He's his own man, always has been.'

'Or is it that you are your own man, perhaps?' she asked with a gentle smile.

Gregor grinned. 'Perhaps. Would you like to have a coffee with me?'

'I've just had one, thanks.'

'Well, have another one. Not here, though.'

'No?'

'No. We'll go somewhere more

interesting. What do you say?'

'Thank you,' she said with another smile. 'I'd like that.'

6

Gregor led the way to a shop across the road from the cathedral. At the front it was full of Orkney knitwear — jumpers and hats, scarves and cardigans. They made their way past them towards the back of the shop, past overflowing shelves of jams and chutneys, books and souvenirs. Fiddle music was playing in the background.

Emma chuckled and whispered, 'Aladdin's Cave!'

'Indeed,' Gregor said, grinning over his shoulder.

The shop was a very long building, and at the back was a restaurant that served local produce and baked goods, homemade cakes and biscuits, full meals even. A woman behind one of the counters was painstakingly icing a cake.

'They make it all here?' Emma asked.

'Most of it, I think.' Gregor pointed

to a spare table. 'Sit yourself down. I'll order some coffee. Or perhaps you'd prefer tea?'

'Will it be Orkney coffee?'

'Och, aye!' he said with a grin. 'The real thing. Grown and processed on the islands. And a cake, will it be?'

She shook her head. 'Just coffee, thanks.'

What a nice man he is, she thought happily as she watched Gregor make his way through the cluttered space to the counter. *It's so good to have met him again. I was starting to feel a bit lonely up here on the edge of the world.*

'They'll bring the coffees over,' Gregor said when he returned.

Emma nodded. 'This is a really interesting place. They seem to do everything here.'

'Yes, they do. It's been going quite a while, as well. Janet, the owner, is a real Jack-of-all-trades. She even designs some of the Fair Isle sweaters herself.'

'How wonderful. Her stuff must sell, too, if she's been in business here a long time.'

'Yes, I think it does. That's not too surprising. We get lots of visitors to the islands, and they all want a bit of Orkney to take home with them. Tourists from all over the world — America and Japan, Canada and the Scandinavian countries. Even some from England!'

'So Orkney is on the world map?'

'It is, most definitely.'

She could sense that was true, sitting here in this cluttered, atmospheric little cafe, surrounded by so much Orcadian produce, and so many reminders of Orkney culture and history.

'Now, to business,' Gregor said, leaning forward and frowning. 'Tell me what you're doing here, Emma. It's not really a holiday, is it?'

She shook her head and began to explain. He listened intently, smiling when she told him again of her encounter with Alastair.

'So what will you do with the house?' he asked when she had finished. 'Do you know yet?'

She shook her head again. 'Not really. Not finally, that is. I imagine I'll give instructions for it to be sold eventually, but I'm not ready to do that just yet.'

'Because . . . ?'

'Well, it's a little difficult to explain,' she admitted with a sheepish smile. 'My head's in a bit of a whirl. I'm still getting used to the idea that I'm the owner of this great big deserted house that I'd never seen until a couple of days ago. Until a couple of months ago I'd never even heard of it.'

'So you want to take your time. Is that it?'

She gave him a rueful smile. 'Well, not all of it. That's just part of it.'

'Is the rest something to do with your aunt, perhaps?'

'Yes,' she admitted with surprise. 'Yes, it is. You see, I never met her, and I know next to nothing about her. Nor does anyone in my family. Yet she left me her house. I'd like to know why. I'd also like to learn something about her while I'm here. I'm beginning to think she must have been an interesting woman.'

Gregor nodded. Then he said, 'What do you think of the coffee?'

'The coffee?' Puzzled by the change of subject, she frowned and said, 'It's good, very nice.'

'Your aunt liked it, too.'

'My aunt . . . ?' she said, staring at him with surprise.

'She used to come in here from time to time, when she was shopping in Kirkwall or going about her business.'

'You knew her?'

He nodded. 'Now, Emma, what are you doing this afternoon? Anything planned?'

'Not really. Not at all, in fact.'

'Good. Would you like to come with me to see some sights? I've got a job to do.'

'Yes,' she said with a smile. 'I'd love to.'

7

They set off in Gregor's Land Rover, which seemed an ideal vehicle for him to have if he really needed all the equipment that was piled in the back.

'Does all that stuff go with you everywhere?' Emma asked, peering around at the mountain of gear.

'Pretty well,' Gregor said. 'I like to be ready to change plan and seize the moment, if the opportunity appears. I might go off to film puffins, but then a pair of humpback whales appears and I want to capture their singing. You just never know.'

'Sound equipment as well? How fascinating,' Emma said. 'What a wonderful job you have.'

'It's not bad,' he conceded.

'Does somebody employ you, or are you freelance?'

'Employ me?' he said with a chuckle.

'Oh, no! I'm far too unreliable — in some people's eyes, at least. You've got it. I'm freelance.'

'So where are we going now, and what do you have in mind?'

'Stenness. It won't take me more than a few minutes. I just want to check that a time-lapse camera I set up there is working OK.'

'That's a camera that takes photos automatically, isn't it? Every hour or two?'

Gregor nodded. 'I'm watching some mallards with it. As I say, it won't take me long, and it gives me the opportunity to show you an interesting part of the island.'

A guided visit — by an expert? Emma was thrilled. She couldn't have hoped for anything like this.

'How far is it?'

'Stenness? Oh, ten or twelve miles. We'll be there in fifteen minutes.'

Nowhere would be very far, she supposed. That was an advantage of living on a fairly small island. Then she corrected herself. Not so small, actually. The maps she had studied had shown Mainland to be far and away the biggest island in Orkney. Most of the others were tiny, miniscule even, and seldom with more than a few homesteads. Mainland was the only one with towns.

'Do you visit the other islands much?' she asked.

'I do. They all have their attractions for someone like me. Birds or whales, or whatever.'

'And are they all inhabited — by people, I mean?'

'No, far from it. There are about seventy islands altogether, and twenty have people living on them. There used to be more, but that's how it is now.'

'Are some of those you visit really remote?'

'Very much so. And for someone like me, that's not a bad thing. Wildlife often prefers places without people. Not always, but often enough.'

By then they had left Kirkwall well

behind and were approaching another small town. 'Where's this?' Emma asked.

'Finstown.'

She saw a couple of shops and an art gallery as they drove past, along the edge of the water, but not much else. It was pretty enough, though, she thought, with wonderful views out to sea.

'What do you know about my aunt?' she asked, returning to the question that intrigued her most.

'Not a lot, but I did know her. We spoke when we met. She would ask me about my work, and tell me the latest news about some archaeological dig she had been following.'

'Goodness! At her age?'

'I suppose she was quite elderly,' he said with a thoughtful frown, 'but I didn't think of her that way. She was always very lively, and interested in all sorts of things. She talked to a good many people, and enjoyed a laugh. Young at heart, I suppose you could say. Actually, she was quite a significant person in Orkney, a sort of local celebrity. Lots of people knew her, or knew of her, which is not too surprising. She lived here many years.'

'Doing what?'

'Oh, she had a keen interest in local history, and Orkney landscapes and wildlife. Everything Orcadian, really. I talked to her and I heard her on the radio occasionally, and I read her books.'

'She wrote books?'

'Yes, popular books about local life and customs, history and one thing or another. She made her living as a freelance journalist — a kindred spirit!' he added, with a sideways grin. 'She was a very busy lady, and seemed to have been so all her life.'

Emma was astonished by these revelations. She shook her head and said, 'I never knew any of that. Nothing at all! Nor did my parents. I'm amazed — and amazed we didn't know. She wasn't born here; I knew that much. So somebody in the family must have known her when she was young. But it's as if by coming here she just fell off the family map, and . . . and disappeared. I can't believe it.'

Gregor was quiet for a few thoughtful moments. Then he said, 'I wonder if that was what she wanted all along, to distance herself from her family? Or perhaps it just worked out that way. The passage of time created a gulf, maybe.'

They were good questions, Emma thought. She would love to know the answers herself. Perhaps she would be able to discover them during her time here.

They slowed and turned on to a smaller road. She saw a huge stone, a rock pillar, twenty feet high, beside the road. There were other similar stones in a nearby field. And suddenly there was water on both sides of the road, open swathes of it stretching away into the distance that for the moment were perfectly still in a shimmering light. The beauty and sheer unexpectedness of the view was stunning. Emma shivered with delight.

'The Stones of Stenness,' Gregor

said. 'We're running along an isthmus now, with the Loch of Stenness on the left-hand side, and the Loch of Harray on the right. It's an important area both archaeologically and for wildlife.'

'Those stones . . . ?' she began.

'Part of a complex of great spiritual significance developed in the Neolithic age.' Gregor glanced at her and added, 'Five or six thousand years ago.'

'Really? As old as that? Like Stonehenge?'

He nodded. 'Like it, yes. But older.'

'I never knew there was anything like that here,' she said, deeply impressed.

Gregor slowed and pointed off to the side. 'Just there, they've been excavating for the past few summers. The archaeologists reckon they've found the remains of the biggest roofed Neolithic building ever discovered in Europe. Some are calling it a Neolithic cathedral.'

They drove on a little way, passing a large group of standing stones arranged in a circle. 'That's the Ring of Brodgar.'

Gregor paused before adding, 'Another part of the complex that we still know so little about.'

He turned into a car park that was part hidden by hummocky grassland. 'This is where I needed to come. I've got my camera set up just over there. I'll check it's working OK, and then we can walk up to the stone circle, if you like.'

'Yes, please. I'd love to do that.'

The camera was set up to cover a reed patch at the edge of the Loch of Harray. Emma watched for a few moments as Gregor checked it, and then she turned to gaze around at the sparse, lonely landscape. The narrow strip of low-lying and gently undulating grassland, almost a small prairie, stretched away into the distance. It was bracketed by the two lochs, expanses of grey water that had lost their sheen now. A stiff breeze had suddenly appeared to ruffle the surface of the water, and make the tall grasses alongside wave and rustle.

She shivered, but not because she

was cold. It was the atmosphere. There was something about this austere and ancient place that touched her deeply, and commanded respect and awe. It was indescribably lonely now, but once there had been people, perhaps many people, toiling here to erect these gaunt monuments. Who were they, and why did they do it? She wondered if anyone would ever know.

'Everything all right?' she asked with a smile when Gregor returned to her side.

'Oh, yes. The camera is working fine. Now let's go see the Ring of Brodgar.'

A timber boardwalk led them out of the car park and onto the road. On the other side of the road, they followed a trail up the gentle slope to the big circle of standing stones. The individual stones, spaced at intervals of about five yards, were massive slabs of rock. Some were twelve or fifteen feet high, others less than that. One or two had been ruined by erosion, and now were not much more than remnants.

Emma stood with Gregor, and for a few moments they gazed around in silence. Only the wind, now quite strong, disturbed the tranquillity of the place, sighing and ruffling the surface of the grass across the circle.

'What's known about all this?' Emma asked at last.

'Not a lot. There are thirty-six stones here now, but it's believed there were sixty originally. Erosion has wrecked some of those that remain, as you can see, and all of them are heavily weathered after standing in the wind and rain for five thousand years.'

'Even so,' Emma said thoughtfully, 'to still be here at all, after all that time . . .'

Gregor nodded. 'I don't suppose anything built in our lifetime will last a fraction of that time — apart from used nuclear fuel dumps.'

'What were the stones used for?'

'Nobody knows for sure. The Neolithic people left no written records, unfortunately. So it's a matter of conjecture.

But it's generally believed that this is a place of great spiritual significance, as is the whole of the surrounding area. People must have come from far and wide to be part of whatever went on here.'

'And they must have come from far and wide to build it in the first place?'

Gregor nodded. 'I'm sure that's right. It would have taken a colossal effort to quarry these stones and bring them to this place. I should imagine the work was spread over many generations, rather like the building of York Minster and Canterbury Cathedral.'

They began to walk round the stone circle, mostly in silence again. There was nothing more to be said. Nothing more was known. It was a time for experiencing, not for talking.

'Thank you for bringing me here, Gregor,' Emma said at last, as they headed back down to the car park. 'It's wonderful.'

'I hoped you'd think so.' He smiled and added, 'Now let's find something to eat. There's a good restaurant I know of not too far from here.'

8

The next day they met for lunch in Kirkwall again. This time it was at a hotel facing the harbour. Gregor said the food was good there, even though the place looked a bit rundown.

'Lots of choice when it comes to seafood,' he said. 'But we can always go round the corner to a chip shop, if you prefer.'

Emma laughed and assured him that lemon sole would be her choice, as well as his.

Gregor was very much at home here, she thought happily, watching him as he stood at the counter waiting to order their meals and drinks. People spoke to him. He smiled and shared a word with one or two. Well, why not? It was his home town. He should feel at home.

For her, it was different. People were pleasant enough. They made eye contact and smiled. They helped when they could, and when she needed help. But she just didn't know anybody. That was the problem, that and not knowing how things worked and where things were. There was no going to Bainbridge's or Fenwick's, she thought with a smile, if you ran out of make-up or knicker elastic!

How on earth had Aunt Freda managed? Mail-order, probably. It would be different now, though, with the internet. Much easier.

Even so, simple matters were surprisingly difficult — or different, at least. Calling into the newsagent's shop that morning here in Kirkwall, for example, looking for a newspaper. That had been an eye-opener. She hadn't been able to spot the paper she wanted. In fact, she hadn't been able to see any of the usual national newspapers, or Scottish papers either.

When she inquired, the woman behind the counter said, 'They're not in yet. Twelve o'clock is the time.'

69

'For what?'

'For when they arrive,' the woman said with a weary smile, as if she was well used to visitors imagining it was the same here as in London or Edinburgh.

Emma smiled herself now, thinking she was on a steep learning curve.

'What?' Gregor demanded as he arrived back at their table. 'What's funny?'

'Oh, I was just thinking how different it is here to what I'm used to. Buying a newspaper in the morning, for example.'

'Can't be done.'

'So I've discovered!' she said with a chuckle.

'It was even worse the other day.'

'Oh?'

'The papers had missed the boat. It was half-three in the afternoon when they arrived.'

She laughed. 'Thank goodness for the internet, eh?'

'Indeed.' He handed her the glass of wine she had asked for. 'Now, what have you decided to do about the house?'

She shook her head. 'Nothing, as yet.

70

I'm still looking around it, and still thinking about Freda.'

Gregor nodded. 'All day, every day?'

'Basically,' she admitted. 'It's supposed to be a bit of a holiday as well, but I can't get Aunt Freda out of my mind.'

'What about tomorrow?'

'What about it?'

'I'm planning on spending an hour or two on the Brough of Birsay. Fancy coming with me for a look around?'

'What is it? Where is it?'

'It's a part-time island just off Birsay. When the tide is out, you can walk across a causeway to it.'

'That sounds interesting. Yes, I'd like to see it. I won't be interfering with your work, though, will I?'

He shook his head. 'I need to call on my brother as well. What if I do that first, and then pick you up about two? That would be just right for the tide.'

'Lovely. You do know where I'll be, don't you?'

'Broch House? Oh, yes, I know where that is.'

'If you forget, ask your brother. He knows,' Emma added with a giggle.

'The last thing I'd do is ask Ally for advice about anything. If it was directions I wanted, he would soon be arguing that I should be going somewhere else instead.'

'You seem to know him very well,' she said mischievously.

'Oh, yes! Yes, indeed.'

'Then I shall hope he doesn't deter you from visiting me tomorrow.'

'No fear of that,' Gregor said with a grin.

★   ★   ★

Emma devoted the next morning to further exploration of Broch House, and made some interesting discoveries. She found a small room, more a big walk-in cupboard really, that she hadn't been in before. It contained floor-to-ceiling shelving full of box files and cartons. Some of the files she opened had records to do with the house. She nodded with satisfaction and continued looking.

It was soon clear that Aunt Freda had been meticulous in recording and keeping information to do with repairs and maintenance, as well as the bills for such things as electricity and the telephone. Over the years, an awful lot of documentation had built up: bills and invoices for roof repairs, plumbing problems, rewiring, extra electrical sockets, and so on. All the usual items, Emma supposed, that any house owner would need to tackle. It made her feel guilty about never taking much interest in her parents' home. Somehow it had never really occurred to her that things had to be done and paid for. All she was used to doing was phoning the landlord when there was a problem in her rented flat.

Other shelves contained a lot of pamphlets, booklets and even a few bigger books that Aunt Freda herself had apparently authored, giving substance to Gregor's comments about her status as a distinguished observer of the local scene. Emma smiled, intrigued by the idea of being related to an author. What would her parents have to say about that? It was astonishing that Mum, at least, hadn't known.

One booklet by Freda Nicholson was about the Stones of Stenness, where Emma had been with Gregor. She laid that aside to read at her leisure. There were also other archaeological sites that Freda had taken an interest in. Goodness! There were so many of them. She hadn't realised that Orkney was such a rich stomping ground for archaeologists.

There were plenty of photographs, too, some in albums and others loose, waiting to be filed. Many were to do with archaeological sites. Pictures of people scraping away in trenches, and some of people triumphantly holding up for camera what they had found. Freda had obviously spent a great deal of time and effort researching the ancient history of Orkney.

One album of photos seemed spectacularly out of place, as well as out of time. Young men in some sort of uniform gazed at the camera with smiles. They were not Orkney men, though. Far from it. These were dark-haired men, quite possibly with a darker complexion than anyone Emma had seen on the island. Studying the photographs, she wondered if they were holiday snaps, perhaps taken in Greece or Spain. The Mediterranean, anyway, or possibly the Middle East. North Africa even? Possibly foreign archaeological digs. There was no reason to think Freda had confined her activities to Orkney. What Emma could see of the landscapes in the background didn't look very much like anywhere she herself had been on her holiday travels. There was a lot of grass, for one thing. And a lot of cloud in the sky.

Then she found photos of what looked like a construction site. Men were working, hauling and carrying, hammering and sawing. What on earth?

This certainly wasn't a holiday scene. Or an archaeological dig either. It was more like a construction site. She stared hard, wondering what had interested Freda in this scene.

A few photos were of one man in particular. Why did he seem so familiar? She frowned. She thought she had seen that photo, that face, somewhere else. Perhaps in a frame hanging on a wall somewhere in the house?

It occurred to her that she still had no idea what Freda had looked like. She began to hunt along the shelves for an album that might show her. At first she had no success; at least, she didn't think so. Freda couldn't have been a vain woman. There were none of the usual portraits that young women liked to take of themselves.

But then she did notice that the same woman appeared in many of the photos of archaeological sites. She was tall and slim. Quite old — perhaps a woman in her sixties. Grey hair. Spectacles. Very upright. Not exactly stern-looking, but not jolly either. A serious woman, who took what she was about seriously. It had to be Freda, Emma decided. Freda in her mature years. There were no photos that might have been of her as a young woman.

She put some of the photos aside for further study. Then she glanced at her watch and saw with astonishment that Gregor would be here any moment. She had better leave all this and get ready for him.

9

The Brough of Birsay was a fifteen-minute walk from Broch House. To save time, bearing the tide table in mind, they drove to the car park overlooking the island.

'It looks wonderful,' Emma said, eyeing the pedestrian causeway cautiously. 'How long have we got?'

'A couple of hours. Time enough for us to get across and walk around the island. The cliffs on the seaward side are worth seeing. Come on!'

They made their way down to the little beach and the start of the causeway. The path was still wet from the withdrawal of the sea, and care had to be taken to avoid slipping on the greasy surface of the stones.

'I'd noticed this island from a window of the house,' Emma said. 'Does anyone live here?'

'Not now, but they used to. There's the remains of a Pictish settlement just over there. Then the Vikings came and built their own village on top of it, complete with a cathedral. Later, the Earls had a place here, before one of them built his palace in the village on the mainland.'

The Earls, she gathered, had been the Norse nobility who for many centuries had owned and occupied Orkney.

'That's the place that's now in ruins? The Earl's Palace?'

Gregor nodded and grinned. 'It's just been one thing after another, in this part of the world!'

'So it seems.'

They reached the end of the causeway and headed up a broad track onto the island. 'This is where the Vikings used to launch their boats,' Gregor told her, 'and then pull them back out of the water to safety, after they'd finished raiding and pillaging — or whatever it was they did.'

All a long time ago, Emma thought,

but Gregor spoke of such things as if they had occurred just yesterday. People here seemed to have long memories. Gregor wouldn't be the only one.

They wandered through the remains of the Norse village, past the ruined church and what some believed had been a monastic building. Then they set off along a path around the perimeter of the island, cliffs appearing and getting bigger the further they went. The island was tilted, Emma realised, sloping upwards from the causeway, so that the cliffs on the seaward side were a good couple of hundred feet high.

There were birds seemingly everywhere: overhead, standing in groups on the grass, sweeping out over the wild waves crashing onto the rocks below. In the distance, to the south, there were even higher cliffs on the mainland. The views in all directions were breathtaking, stunning.

'How are you getting on at the house?' Gregor asked suddenly.

'Oh, I'm still exploring the place and

discovering what's there. It's a big house, especially for just one person. I can't believe Aunt Freda lived there all alone. It's also very interesting. I'd come to think there was no longer anything of a personal nature in the house, but just this morning I found a storage room full of paperwork — accounts, bills, and so on. I don't believe Aunt Freda ever threw anything away, bless her. There are photographs, too. Lots of photos of what look like archaeological digs. Perhaps you could look at them when we get back? You might be able to shed some light on them.'

'Any of Freda herself?'

'Some, I assume, are of her, and friends and colleagues. Maybe you'll recognise some of them. Mind you, they're mostly from years ago. None of them look very recent. None that I've found so far, at least.'

'I'd be interested to take a look. Now, if you'll excuse me, I want to take some photos from here of the sea cliffs. I want them to illustrate an article I'm working on for a birding magazine.'

'Oh? You're a writer, too?'

'After a fashion.' He grinned and added, 'When I can't avoid it. Jack-of-all-trades, me. But photography's my main thing. That and camera work, of course.'

She watched as Gregor got to work, moving perilously close to the edge of the cliffs. From there was a good view of a neighbouring cliff wall with extraordinary rock formations. The wall was like a multi-layered cake, with thin horizontal slabs of sandstone piled high on top of each other, all the way from the sea-washed bottom to the mist-wreathed summit.

'They're flagstones,' Gregor explained when he rejoined her. 'Caithness flags. In the nineteenth century there was a roaring trade in exporting stone from this part of the world, all of it destined for people to walk on in the growing English towns and cities.'

'It's extraordinary — and quite beautiful, in its own way,' Emma said thoughtfully. 'I've never seen anything like it.'

Gregor smiled and took more photographs. He knew this land well, and seemed to be enjoying showing her it.

They completed their circuit of the island and headed back down to the causeway. 'How much longer have you got here?' Gregor asked.

'A few days. Another week, perhaps, but I have to be back at work a week on Monday.'

'Are you going to be able to get everything done in that time?'

'I'll have to!' she said with a laugh.

It was a question she hadn't really considered. So far, she had been on a voyage of discovery, and after a rocky start had begun to enjoy herself. Orkney hadn't been a place she had really wanted to come to, but now that she was here it was proving to be surprisingly interesting.

Gregor was helping a lot, of course. She would have had no idea where, or what, anything was without him. It was very good of him to spend so much time showing her around. She sensed that he was as happy in her company as she was in his. Beyond that, thought, she didn't let herself go. A week on Monday was much too far into the future.

As they set off back to Broch House, Emma gave voice to something that had been puzzling her. 'I wonder why Aunt Freda never married,' she said thoughtfully.

'She can't have met anyone she liked enough, can she?'

'No, probably not.'

'Perhaps she was happy with her life just the way it was.'

'Mm. You're probably right,' Emma mused. 'She must have been. Otherwise she wouldn't have stayed here, would she?' She considered further, and added, 'I mean, she didn't belong here, did she? Not originally.'

'I don't think so. Unless any other members of the family are from Orkney?' he said, glancing sideways at her.

'That's a point.' She frowned. 'I've

not heard of anyone else in the family living here, or coming from here. No, I don't think there's a family connection. I'm not aware of one, at least.'

Gregor changed gear and slowed down while he encouraged a wandering cow to leave the road and hurry back through an open gate into its field. 'So how did your aunt end up here?' he asked.

'Do you know,' she said slowly, 'I really have no idea. None at all. But it's an interesting question.'

'Another one,' Gregor added, 'is how Freda is related to you. Do you know?'

'Well, I think she was my mother's aunt, not mine. So she must have been my great-aunt.'

'Then why wasn't the house left to your mother?'

Emma shook her head. 'I have no idea. But it's something to think about, isn't it?'

10

'You've never been inside Broch House before, I take it?' Emma asked.

Gregor shook his head. 'No. I didn't really know your aunt in a personal or social sense. She was just someone whose name and face were familiar, and who I used to bump into and chat with from time to time.'

'But you used to speak to her?'

'Just hello and good morning; maybe a word or two about the weather, and what we were both up to. That was about all.'

Emma was disappointed. She had hoped it had been more than that. 'Would you like to see around the house now?'

'Very much. Thank you.'

They paused inside the garden gate while Gregor cast his eye around the garden. 'This is good,' he said with a nod of appreciation.

'You think so? It's a bit bare for my taste. Not much colour.'

Gregor laughed. 'You have no idea about gardening in Orkney, do you? Very few people even have a garden worth the name. Surely you've noticed that?'

'Well, now that you mention it, I suppose I have. It's surprising how many houses are surrounded only by grass or a patch of gravel. I just assumed it was the time of year.'

'The wind and the culture, more like it,' Gregor said, shaking his head. 'We don't really have much of a gardening tradition anywhere in the Northern Isles, but it is perfectly possible to have a garden. Freda has done a lot of work here,' he added. 'Just look! The perimeter hedge gives the protection you need from the wind. And there are trees, too. They're a rarity on Orkney. Even more so on Shetland.' He gazed admiringly at the two big sycamores on either side of the gate.

'I had noticed them, I suppose,' Emma admitted. 'As you say, there seem to be very few trees anywhere on the island.'

'That's right. So Freda developed a little sheltered oasis here. No doubt you'll see all sorts of herbaceous perennials — flowering plants — coming through, as we get into summer. This garden is worth a lot in Orkney terms.'

Emma took a fresh look around her and decided that perhaps there was more here than met the eye at first glance. 'I'll take your word for it,' she said dubiously. 'There's not much colour here now, though.'

'But there will be,' Gregor promised. 'The shrubs in the hedge will soon be in blossom. But come on! Show me inside the house.'

They moved into the hallway. 'I see what you mean,' he said as they stood together. 'It is a big house, isn't it? How many bedrooms did you say?'

'Six. They're all furnished, but I

don't think they were all in use.'

'Obviously. Unless Freda had lots of visitors, or she liked to use them in rotation.'

Emma shook her head. 'I don't think so. I just don't know what she wanted with a house this big.'

'It's in very tidy condition,' Gregor remarked thoughtfully. 'She must have had help looking after it. A cleaner, perhaps.'

Emma nodded. 'Yes. At least a cleaner and a gardener, for the last few years anyway.'

'We should find out who they were.'
'We?'

'Sorry,' Gregor said ruefully. 'I meant you. I'm being presumptuous.'

'Not at all!' Emma said, laughing. 'I'm teasing. You're just as curious as I am, aren't you? Aunt Freda really is a mystery. Anyway, I'm glad. I'd appreciate any help you can give me.'

'Glad we've got that settled,' Gregor said with a grin.

'Let's do a quick walkabout. Then I'll

show you the photographs I found.'

Emma was delighted that Gregor seemed as interested as she was in finding out more about Freda. Apart from the fact that he was an Orcadian who knew his way around, she liked him. She liked him a lot. He was a kindly and interesting man. Good company, too.

If only he wasn't married! she thought wistfully. Unfortunately, all the best men were. *Just my luck*, she thought again, only half in jest. *I find a lovely man for once, and what do you know? He wears a ring on his wedding finger! Let it be a warning: don't let him come too close. Keep him at a safe distance.*

All the same, she wasn't going to turn down his offer of help. Maybe together they could sort out what she needed to know about Aunt Freda. She certainly wasn't going to put the house up for sale until she had done that.

'So, the photos,' Gregor said when they had done the rounds. 'Let's have a look at them.'

She took him to the storage room.

'I'm beginning to think of this as the archive,' she said. 'There's so much here.'

'I see what you mean.' Gregor looked around, fascinated. 'Everything so well organised, too. Mind you, I shouldn't be surprised about that. Your aunt always struck me as a serious and fastidious person.'

'Not much like me, then,' Emma said with a sigh.

'Oh, you can't say that until you've accumulated as much stuff as Freda had. If you had, you wouldn't want it all in a pile on the floor. You would want to know where things were, and to be able to lay your hands on them when you needed them. All us freelancers have to be well organised, or we'd soon go under.'

'I'm not too sure about that, Gregor. I might have just put it all in the bin.'

'Tut, tut! I'm sure you wouldn't. You're far too sensible a person. Now, what have we here?'

She showed him an album that

seemed mostly to be a record of archaeological digs. He recognised some of the sites, which were spread around several of the islands. People were scrupulously digging and scraping, sieving soil and sometimes just standing watching.

'You must have to be a very patient person to do this,' Emma suggested.

Gregor nodded. 'That's Freda, by the way,' he said, pointing to a tall, very upright woman wearing glasses who was standing alongside a deep trench.

Emma peered at the photo. 'Yes, I thought that must be her. She's very distinctive.'

'Very. These were obviously taken a long time ago, but she stayed like that the rest of her life. She never looked any older than she does here. And she was always the kind of person you couldn't pass in the street without wondering who she was.'

A bit like you, Gregor! Emma thought automatically. Strange how some people had that special quality about them.

Was it charisma? Something like that. Anyway, Gregor definitely had it. She had seen that the first time he had spoken to her.

She reached for another album and opened it. This was the one with what she thought of as the construction collection. Black and white photographs. Men busy building something. They were hammering and sawing, lifting and carrying, perched on ladders.

'A hive of industry!' she said with a chuckle. 'Also from a long time ago. Looking at the men, I wondered if the photos were taken somewhere around the Mediterranean. Perhaps it was an archaeological site in Greece, or somewhere like that.'

Together they pored over a couple of the photographs.

'Ah!' Gregor said, leaning closer and chuckling. 'I know exactly where this is — and I know what they're all doing, as well. But I've never seen these photos before. They're wonderful.' He straightened up, turned, and smiled at her with an infuriatingly smug expression.

'You know where it is?' she said impatiently. 'Come on, then — tell me.'

'I can do better than that. I can take you there right now. Come on! Get your coat.'

11

'So where are we going now?' Emma asked.

'You'll see,' Gregor said with a mischievous grin. 'Have patience.'

They drove down through the village of Twatt, on past the lochs of Stenness and Harray, through Finstown, and on to Kirkwall. On the way, they talked about the archaeological sites in the photographs.

'Freda seems to have been involved in all the big ones over the past forty or fifty years,' Gregor said, shaking his head. 'It's amazing what that woman did.'

'She must have had a lot of spare time,' Emma said, disgruntled by the mystery of where she was being taken, and by Gregor's refusal to tell her where they were going.

'As a freelance journalist? A magazine writer?' Gregor mused. 'I don't know if she would have had a lot of spare time. It's a demanding way to make a living. What she must have had was a good nose for a story. Freelancers need that.'

'Maybe she was just colossally rich.'

'Is your family rich? Do you have that in your background?'

She sniggered. 'Not really. My dad would probably take great offence if anyone presumed he was. He's worked very hard for what he and Mum have.'

'Doing what?'

'Oh, nothing glamorous. He worked for an engineering firm on Tyneside, before it went bust and he had to take early retirement.'

'That must have been an interesting career.'

'Well, he liked it. And it paid the bills, including the mortgage for the family home in Gosforth, where Mum and Dad still live.'

'And you, too?'

She shook her head. 'I have my own place, a flat just over the river in

Gateshead. It's in a converted ware-house that was part of an ironworks in the olden days.'

'Like it there?'

'It's pretty good. Handy for the town centre, and for work. I won't stay there forever, but it's ideal at the moment. What about you?'

'Oh, I have a flat here in Kirkwall.'

She was about to ask for more information when she realised they had passed through Kirkwall already, and now were leaving it behind.

'Where to now?'

'It's not far. Five minutes, ten at the most.'

'Then what will I see?'

He just grinned.

'You know, you can be a really infuriating man?'

His grin grew wider. 'I know,' he admitted. 'You're not the first person to tell me that.'

They drove though a small village along the water's edge, a line of traditional stone cottages and a modern retirement complex that looked like a beach resort somewhere more exotic. 'St Mary's,' Gregor informed her. 'And that's Scapa Flow on the right. In both world wars it was the Royal Navy's main naval base. That was where they kept the battleships and the cruisers — all the big ships — until they were needed.'

'Isn't it too remote? They were a long way from the action, surely?'

'Well, the thing with battleships was that you rarely used them. Mostly you wanted them on call, as a sort of deterrent, and while they were at rest they had to be somewhere safe. In its wisdom, the Admiralty thought Scapa Flow was a good place. Apart from the time in 1939, six weeks after the war started, when a U-boat got through.'

'What happened then?'

'A battleship, the *Royal Oak*, was sunk. Eight hundred men drowned, and the U-boat got away.'

Emma grimaced and straightened up to peer ahead. The road curved and ran on a long bridge out across the water. As they reached the entrance, she saw the way ahead was just two lanes of tarmac, with railings on either side.

'Goodness! Where are we going?'

'This is the first of the Churchill Barriers,' Gregor said. 'After the sinking of the *Royal Oak*, the Prime Minister ordered barriers to be built between the islands on the east side of Scapa Flow, to prevent it ever happening again.'

'Hence, the Churchill Barriers?'

He nodded. 'Exactly. They worked, too. But in the long run the really important thing about them was the road that was built along the top of them. You can drive all the way down to the tip of South Ronaldsay now. Previously you'd have been faced with umpteen short boat trips between the islands.'

They crossed the first of the barriers in a minute or two. Almost immediately, Gregor turned left and drove a little way up a track towards a small building on a slight rise.

'And this is?'

'The Italian Chapel. Have you heard of it?'

She shook her head.

'There's a lovely story behind it. Many of the men who built the Churchill Barriers were Italian prisoners of war, captured in North Africa and sent to camps here. This one was called Camp Sixty.'

'What a shock Orkney must have been for them!'

'It must have been, but I don't think it was entirely unwelcome. At least here they were out of the war, and safe. I don't suppose many of them hankered after being back on the front line in the desert.'

'Ah! Wait a minute.' The penny had dropped. 'So were they the men in those photographs of Freda's?'

'Yes. They were building what you see in front of you now. They wanted to have a little piece of home here with them, so they asked the commandant for permission to build their own chapel. He gave it, and much else besides, and they got to work, mostly using scrap materials. Come on,' he added, 'let's look inside.'

They got out of the car and started walking. As they neared the building, Emma squinted at it and laughed. From the front it was a typical small Italian church, but that was only part of the story.

'It's just an old hut!' she cried with amusement.

'Indeed it is. An old Nissen hut. Two, actually, I believe. The prisoners were given them and told to get on with it.'

Gregor pulled open the door and ushered Emma inside. She stepped forward and stopped in her tracks, marvelling at what she could see. 'It's beautiful,' she said with astonishment, taking in the painted walls, the altarpiece and everything else.

'All, or most of it, made from scrap materials, remember? There was a war on. Materials of every sort were in short supply.'

She wandered around, marvelling at the artistry on display, and at the depth of feeling that so clearly had gone into the design and execution of the work. It was a place of love and dedication, all accomplished so long ago by men so far from home.

Gregor let her wander alone for a few minutes. When she was ready, she turned and nodded to him. He smiled and led the way back outside.

'Thank you for bringing me here,' she said, putting her arm in his without even registering that she was doing it.

'You're very welcome,' he said softly back. 'Most visitors find it a moving experience, especially if they know nothing in advance.'

'So Freda saw what was going on,' she said thoughtfully, 'and wanted to make some sort of photographic record of the work in progress? Perhaps write about it, too?'

'It looks that way.'

'How clever of you, Gregor, to identify the site. I would never have known this place existed.'

He nodded complacently. 'The tricky question,' he suggested, 'is to know how Freda came to be here at all. It was a POW camp, remember? A war was raging. People were dying in their millions. Secrecy was draconian, as was security. How come Freda was here?'

'You mean, was she here in some official capacity?'

'Well, she could scarcely have got inside a POW camp as a private visitor, could she? Not in wartime.'

'I suppose not, no.'

'It was a very dangerous time. Why, anyway, would a young woman so far from home herself have even wanted to be consorting with the enemy, as I believe the offence was called at the time?'

'Well, perhaps the first question to be asked is how and why Freda was in Orkney at all,' Emma said slowly. 'What was she doing on the island?'

'Yes, indeed,' Gregor said, nodding in agreement. 'We'll get nowhere without knowing the answer to that one.'

12

They got no further with the questions they had raised about Freda. Eventually, Gregor announced that he must be off. He had work to do.

'Oh, of course!' Emma said. 'How selfish of me. I'm keeping you from your work, and from your family.'

He shook his head and said with a smile, 'No, you're not. There's no one waiting for me.'

'Well, I appreciate the help you've given me.'

'I'm as interested in Freda as you are now, Emma, but I'm afraid duty calls. I'll pop by again in a day or two, to see if you've made any further progress.'

He studied her for a moment, and she wondered if he was going to kiss her goodbye. He didn't. With another little smile, he turned and departed, giving her a final wave as he set off in his Land Rover.

Afterwards she sighed and wondered what to do now. She had rather hoped Gregor would stay longer. Without him, it threatened to be a long day. Without him, in fact, she didn't think she would get any further with her enquiries.

Besides, she thought ruefully, she liked his company. He was a very nice man, as well as being so handsome and interesting. It was hard to believe he was the brother of a man like Alastair.

She did wonder, though, why Gregor wore a wedding ring if he wasn't married, and she hoped he had been truthful with her.

By coincidence, just as she was leaving to return to the guesthouse, Alastair put in another of his appearances. She wasn't in the least surprised. In fact, she had half-expected it. Sometimes she wondered if he was keeping an eye on her comings and goings, just so he could catch her at a weak moment and get her to sell Broch

House to him at a knockdown price.

'Has that no-good brother of mine gone?' he demanded in a mock-serious tone.

'I'm afraid he has, Alastair. What can I do for you today?'

'I was just wondering if you were ready yet to put the house on the market. As I told you, I might be interested.'

She shook her head. 'Nothing has been decided yet. Don't worry — I'm sure you'll be one of the first people to see the 'For Sale' sign if and when it goes up.'

'Well, I suppose that can't be far off now. You'll not be wanting to spend much more of your valuable time in a place like this. How long are you planning on staying, by the way?'

'I'm not sure,' she replied, irritated by his questions. 'That's something else that hasn't been decided. As long as it takes, I suppose.'

'Well, don't let that brother of mine distract you. You just concentrate on your main business here.'

'What on earth do you mean?'

'Why, getting this old house on the market! Spring's advancing. Summer's coming. You don't want to leave it too long. The potential buyers will all have found somewhere else.'

'I'll bear that in mind, Alastair. Thank you so much for your advice. Now, if you'll excuse me, I must be on my way.'

'Of course, of course. Time and tide — they wait for none of us, do they?'

He followed her as she made her way towards the car.

'Here's another word of advice,' he said. 'You're best keeping your distance from my brother. Gregor will only disappoint you in the end.'

This was too much! 'I don't know what you're talking about,' Emma said sharply. 'But it might be better to keep your advice to yourself, thank you very much. I really don't need to hear any more of it.'

'Suit yourself, lassie,' he said, turning

away. 'But don't say you've not been warned.'

What an annoying man, she thought unhappily as she turned the ignition to start the engine.

Even so, once she had calmed down she wondered if she might have displayed her interest in Gregor too obviously. She didn't really think so, and nothing had happened between them anyway. But perhaps she ought to be more careful. She didn't want to start any more tongues wagging. Alastair's was bad enough.

In any case, if Gregor had ever indicated any interest at all in her as a person of the female variety, she might well have responded appropriately; but he hadn't. That was the top and bottom of it, she thought ruefully. He simply wasn't interested in her as a woman. And she had done and said nothing to provoke such an interest anyway. They were simply two friendly people who were trying to find answers to a mystery that had intrigued them both. That was all, unfortunately.

She shook her head and got on with a task she needed to do before she left at the end of the week. That was arranging an appointment with a solicitor in Kirkwall to discuss what needed doing about Broch House if and when she put it up for sale. That was still her aim, but it was one without a timetable attached to it as yet.

She was in no hurry now, she reflected. She was reconciled to that. Freda deserved a little more consideration from the family that had lost touch with her, even though she had not forgotten them. If that meant returning to Orkney to deal with unfinished business, well, so be it.

13

Almost before she knew it, Friday came round and it was time for Emma to start the journey home. She left the guesthouse soon after breakfast, quite sad to be going, and headed into Kirkwall. The ferry wouldn't leave from Stromness until later that day, so there was time to kill, and she thought she would spend some of it in the Orkney capital; have a last look around. Part of her even hoped she might bump into Gregor again, although the chances didn't seem good.

They had exchanged phone numbers during their last meeting, but she didn't want to call him to say goodbye again when they had already done that in person. She was mindful of how it might look, and didn't want to risk him regarding her as too pushy. So far as she knew, anyway, it could be a girlfriend who picked up the phone, and she didn't want that either. He had said that there wasn't a wife waiting at home for him, but he wore a wedding ring, and a man like Gregor was bound to have a female somewhere in his life. After all, even his objectionable brother had one!

Emma parked near the harbour for the last time and wandered again up the lane that led into the town centre, stopping on the way for a coffee and to browse in a bookshop. Buying souvenirs and gifts had been a long way from her mind, but she couldn't return home empty-handed. She had to find something to take back with her.

She grew bored with her search and settled for a beautiful book of photographs of the islands for her parents. That would have to do, she decided. Her friends were going to have to do without this time. They would no doubt be returning from Greece fully laden with presents for her and everyone else, but they would understand. She had

had too much on her mind this hectic week.

After that, she decided to have a look around St Magnus Cathedral, the handsome building right in the centre of the town. It was built of a lovely red sandstone, but unfortunately the stone was soft and very vulnerable to Orkney weathering, so the information panels said. Emma guessed that fund-raising to repair the church was pretty much a non-stop process. All the same, it had stood proudly in the centre of Kirkwall for a thousand years, and looked good for plenty more yet.

She read from a leaflet that the cathedral was of Norse origin, dating from a time when both Orkney and Shetland had belonged to Norway. Illustrative wall panels and memorials, and even the grave of an Earl, brought that history home to her as she explored the austere but atmospheric interior. There was even a copy of the Bible in the Old Norse language open for inspection.

In an understated way, the cathedral was very impressive, prompting the thought that before she came here again — which she surely would — she would try to do some reading on Orkney history. She had seen so many historic sites and interesting places in the past week. Yet she knew so little about them, and how they all fitted into the islands' long story. But the brief visit had served to capture her imagination.

Besides, she thought with a rueful smile as she headed out into a thin, watery sunlight, *I must have seemed incredibly ignorant to Gregor. I don't want to be in that position still, if I should ever happen to meet him again.*

⋆   ⋆   ⋆

She paused for a moment to get used to the light. That was when she saw a vaguely familiar face passing by. She stared. The figure paused and looked back. Then recognition dawned. It was Gregor's mother, the old lady she had spoken to on the ferry a week earlier.

'Hello, Mrs McEwan!' she called, giving her a little wave. 'Remember me?'

'Of course!' Mrs McEwan laughed. 'I thought I knew you from somewhere. You were on the ferry from Scrabster, weren't you?'

'That's me.'

'Are you enjoying your holiday?'

'Very much, but sadly it's almost over. I'll be leaving on the ferry this afternoon.'

'So soon? That's a pity. But you've enjoyed your visit, I hope?'

'Oh yes, it's been a very busy and interesting week, Mrs McEwan. I've seen your son, Gregor, once or twice as well. Actually, I've seen both your sons! Alastair lives near where I was staying.'

'Oh, you've been in Birsay, have you?'

'That's right. I even visited the Brough of Birsay one day. It was lovely.'

'Yes, it is. Wild and rugged, but a lovely place. I'm pleased you got there.'

The old lady turned as another woman, this one about Emma's age, bustled up to them. 'Here you are, Jennifer! Let me introduce you to someone I met on the ferry last week, and who now unfortunately is leaving us. Jennifer is my daughter,' she added with a smile at Emma.

'Hello! I'm Emma Mason.'

'Jennifer Gregg,' the other woman said with a friendly smile.

They shook hands.

'We planned to have coffee together,' Mrs McEwan said. 'Would you care to join us, Emma?'

She was uncertain for a moment.

'You would be most welcome,' Jennifer assured her.

'Well, in that case, thank you, I would love to join you. I've got plenty of time before the ferry leaves this afternoon.'

'Oh, any amount!' Mrs McEwan said firmly. 'There's no hurry at all.'

They headed for the shop and restaurant Emma had been to once before with Gregor. They had a friendly conversation there about life in Orkney, and somehow coffee became lunch. Neither of the other women was in a hurry, Emma soon realised. Nor was she, actually. Fresh quiche and salad went down very nicely, and was followed by tea they shared from an especially large teapot.

'You see, Jennifer, I can tell Emma is feeling at home with us already,' Mrs McEwan confided to her daughter. 'She likes the pace of life here.'

'Oh, Mother!' Jennifer said, laughing. 'Don't be such a terrible tease. The poor girl has a long wait for the ferry, that's all. What else could she do, poor thing?'

Emma smiled at the good-natured banter. 'Actually, I've enjoyed my time here. It's been lovely.'

'Will you come again?' Jennifer asked. 'That's always the test.'

'Oh, yes! Certainly. In a few weeks' time, probably.' She went on to explain that she had her aunt's house to sort out, or to do something about. So she needed to return for that, if for no other reason. 'I haven't managed to accomplish as much as I had hoped this week,' she concluded.

'It'll take some sorting, I'm sure,' Jennifer conceded. 'Especially if you've been trying to do it on your own.'

'Well, yes.' Emma hesitated. 'Actually, I haven't been entirely alone. Your brother, Gregor, has been helping me a bit. We met on the ferry,' she added, seeing Jennifer's surprise.

'Oh, good,' Jennifer said.

'Gregor hasn't told me,' Mrs McEwan said, also seeming surprised. 'But, then, I don't know three-quarters of the folk he helps. He's very good that way.'

'He certainly is,' Emma agreed. 'Apart from anything else, he's been able to tell me so much about my aunt, who I never met.'

'How strange,' Jennifer said thoughtfully. 'Then why did she leave you the house?'

Emma shook her head. 'I wish I could tell you,' she admitted. 'That's one of the things I'm hoping to discover.'

'Does the house have a name?' Mrs McEwan asked, seeming to surface from some deep contemplation.

Emma nodded. 'Broch House.'

'Ah!' Mrs McEwan nodded with satisfaction. 'So your aunt was Miss Nicholson, Miss Freda Nicholson?'

'Yes.' Emma smiled with surprise herself now. 'Did you know her?'

'Of course! Everyone knew Freda.'

'Not quite everyone, Mother,' Jennifer added. 'But you're right, she was well-known. A lovely person, too. And so interesting.'

Emma smiled. 'I'm really glad I bumped into you both. Perhaps you can tell me more about her?'

'Certainly we can,' Mrs McEwan said. 'How much time do you have, dear?'

14

Emma didn't learn a lot more from her companions. Mostly, they repeated what she had already learned from Gregor. Over a great many years, Freda had become well-known through her writing and broadcasting on Orkney topics. Neither of them had known Freda in a personal sense, unfortunately, but they were a mine of information about her interest in archaeology, birds, flora, folklore — and everything else to do with Orkney life.

'Gregor said she was a freelance journalist,' Emma told them.

'That sounds right,' Jennifer said. 'Anyway, he would know, wouldn't he? After all, he's much the same himself — freelance, I mean.'

Mrs McEwan gave a heavy sigh and said, 'How I wish my son had found himself a proper job.'

'Oh, I think he has a wonderful job!' Emma protested.

'Doing what, though? Photographing seals and birds, and things? He could be doing something useful — working in a bank or teaching. Even bricklaying! A proper career.'

'Oh, Mother!' Jennifer said. 'Stop teasing. You know you don't really mean that. Gregor is doing very well for himself. I wish I could make a living out of photographing birds. That would suit me very well.'

'Me, too,' Emma added. 'It beats working in an insurance office, like I do.'

'Yes,' Mrs McEwan said, 'Gregor has a lovely time. But if he falls off a cliff and can't work for six months because he's broken his leg, he will have no money coming in, will he? Anyway, I don't suppose he makes a lot of money at the best of times, doing what he does.'

'I'll see if I can get him a job in the office where I work,' Emma suggested.

'Perhaps he would like that better?'

'Now you're talking!' Mrs McEwan said, nodding her head vigorously.

Jennifer burst into laughter. Emma joined her, and after a few moments of token dissent so did Mrs McEwan.

'I do worry about him, though,' the old lady confessed. 'He's never been the same since — '

'Mother!' Jennifer said sharply. 'Please don't start that again.'

Mrs McEwan sighed. Then she added, 'Perhaps a regular job wouldn't suit him very well, but it would ease my mind. I could stop worrying about him then.'

Somehow they seemed to have reached the end of their conversation. Emma sensed it was time to go, and started to make preparations to depart. Mrs McEwan returned to the subject of Freda just before she did so.

'I attended her funeral in St Magnus Cathedral,' she said with some relish. 'It was lovely.'

'Funerals are not lovely,' Jennifer said with exasperation.

'Well, Freda's was,' the old lady said stoutly. 'So many people there! Freda would have been proud of the way they celebrated her life.'

Emma's ears pricked up at this bit of news. 'Was much said of her early life?'

'Not really. Just that she hadn't been born here. I don't think anyone knew much about the time before she came to Orkney.'

'How strange,' Jennifer said with a frown, glancing at Emma. 'Did your family not know about it?'

Emma shook her head. 'I think she simply disappeared from my family's life. My parents seem to know nothing about her. It is odd, you're right. I don't understand it myself.'

Jennifer said she would walk Emma back to the car park, as she was going to collect her own car there in order to give her mother a lift home. 'So you've met Alastair,' she said with a chuckle as they walked along. 'How did you get on with him? He's not everyone's cup of tea.'

Emma laughed. 'He wants to buy my house — Freda's house, that is.'

'For next to nothing?'

'Yes! How did you know? Have you been speaking to Gregor?'

'Not recently, no. I just know what Ally's like. He's the only one in the family with any money, mainly because he hangs on to it so well and is good at finding bargains. I would imagine he's been pointing out all the defects of the house?'

'Oh, yes. I can't imagine why he's interested in it. So far as he's concerned, it should be demolished to stop it being a health and safety risk.'

'That's Alastair!'

'Apparently the Orkney economy is in steep decline, as well.'

'So prices are rock-bottom, and houses hard to sell?'

'Exactly.'

'That really is my brother for you. My advice is to ignore him. Any house Freda Nicholson owned and lived in so long must be wonderful.'

'It is, actually. I really do like it. It's such an interesting place. Mind you, I'm still struggling to find out how Freda lived. That's become an intriguing question, one that your other brother has been helping me with. I think he's now as interested as I am.'

'Gregor. Yes, I can imagine. Here we are! Which is your car?'

'The little Clio, over there in the corner.'

'Oh, that's a nice little car. I would love something like that myself. Instead, I have to drive that great big thumping thing over there!'

Jennifer pointed to a double-cab pickup truck that looked capable of carrying almost anything that anyone might ever want to transport anywhere.

'It must be good when you go shopping,' Emma suggested. 'You'll be able to get everything in one go.'

'Oh, yes — for the whole year!'

They walked together over to Emma's little car. Suddenly, Jennifer seemed to have something in mind that she was finding it a struggle to say.

'What?' Emma said with a smile.

Jennifer laughed and brought her hand up to her face with embarrassment. 'That obvious, is it?'

'That you want to tell me something? Yes, it is. I'm a diligent student of human emotions and psychology. You want to tell me something, but you're not sure how to do it. Don't worry, Jennifer. I'm a big girl now. What have I done wrong?'

'Nothing, absolutely nothing! Oh, dear. I should never have started.' She paused, sighed and then said, 'It's Gregor.'

'Oh?'

'There's something you should know.'

15

Emma steeled herself. She got ready to be told Gregor was a married man, a serial philanderer and that she should keep clear of him to avoid wrecking his family. Maybe she was even about to be accused of being a threat to the family?

'All right, Jennifer. What is it that I need to know? What have I done wrong?'

'Oh, nothing! Nothing at all, Emma, so far as I know. What I feel I should tell you is that ... Well, have you noticed that he wears a wedding ring?'

Emma coloured with embarrassment and guilt. Then she shrugged and said, 'Yes, I have, actually. But that's nothing to do with me. I have no designs on your brother, if that's what you mean, Jennifer.'

'No?'

'No. Nothing at all has happened between us.'

Jennifer stared for a long moment, and then said, 'That's a pity. I was hoping something might have happened. You seem to be exactly the right sort of person a man like Gregor should be meeting.'

'Whatever do you mean? I don't want to find myself in the midst of a family situation, Jennifer. Gregor's a married man, and I am certainly not looking for an affair with a married man. I'm really not that desperate — and not that stupid either.'

'Oh, Emma! Please don't take on so. You've got hold of the wrong end of the stick. Gregor is not a married man. That's the point I wanted to make.'

'Then why does he wear a wedding ring?'

'My brother is a deeply unhappy widower. There, does that make it clearer?'

Emma took a deep breath. Then she shrugged. 'I didn't know that. Not that it makes any difference,' she added. 'Nothing has happened between us.

Gregor has simply been helping me with my research.'

'Well, I still think that's a pity. Maggie has been gone quite a few years now. I don't like to think of him spending the rest of his life alone, which seems to be his intention.'

A gust of wind interrupted their conversation. It brought a cloud of dust, followed by a hint of rain. Both women ducked their heads for a moment. Then Jennifer looked up, smiled and said, 'What a pity you're leaving so soon, Emma. There isn't really time for this now, is there?'

Emma shook her head. There wasn't time, and she didn't have the interest. All this was none of her business anyway.

'I'm sorry if I seemed to be attacking you,' Jennifer said softly. 'I really wasn't, you know.'

'That's all right,' Emma replied awkwardly. 'I'm sorry I was so defensive.'

'We should chat again. Will you come

back to Orkney, do you think?'

'I'll have to. I have Freda's house to settle.'

'Of course. Will you get in touch when you do? Here, let me give you my phone number.' She dug into her pocket and produced a pen and a scrap of paper, which she studied for a moment. 'It's just a receipt from the Co-op,' she decided. 'Nothing I need to keep.' She scribbled for a moment and handed the scrap of paper over. Emma thanked her and turned to get into the car. Jennifer stood where she was while Emma started the engine.

'What happened to Gregor's wife?' Emma couldn't help asking before she put the car in gear.

'Oh, it was very sad. She was killed in a road accident in Africa, for which he blames himself. It really wasn't his fault, but he doesn't see it that way. He thinks he should never have agreed to take her with him.' Jennifer shrugged and added, 'Maggie was hard to deny anything, but he doesn't see it that way.'

'I'm sorry. Thank you for telling me, by the way.'

As Emma drove out of the car park, a glance in the rear-view mirror told her that Jennifer was still watching.

* * *

Waiting for the ferry to sail, and then during the voyage across the Pentland Firth, there was plenty of time to think. Too much time, actually. Emma mulled over what Jennifer had told her. Poor Gregor. What a sad situation.

Not that it made any real difference so far as she was concerned. As she had told Jennifer, nothing had happened between herself and Gregor in a romantic sense, nothing at all. He was a fine man. She liked him a lot, and admittedly would like to see him again — to help with the pursuit of Freda, she added quickly. But that was it. There was no need for Jennifer to get upset — or hopeful either, she thought with a wry smile.

Anyway, from what she had seen, Gregor had a good life here. His work was obviously important to him, and he enjoyed it. It gave him a good living, despite his mother's regret that he didn't have a 'proper' job. She grinned at that thought. Mrs McEwan was a bit of a character, and Emma liked her. She liked Jennifer, too. Perhaps she would see them all again. She hoped so.

Not Alastair, though. She could do without seeing him again. Mind you, she thought, he was a bit of a character, too. What a family they were!

As for Broch House, she didn't know what to do about that. It would have to be sold eventually, of course, but not until she was ready to take the necessary steps. Not until she knew more about Freda, in other words. Not until Gregor had helped her get further down that road.

Then we'll see, she decided. *But for now, at least, I'm going to put it in cold storage. I have a life to lead, too, and work to do. I'd better get on with it.*

16

As she neared Newcastle, Emma couldn't wait to get back home to her flat. The city seemed so drab and crowded after Orkney, and the traffic was terrible. It took an age to get from the northern outskirts through to the Tyne Bridge, and then over the river. It started to rain just as she was unloading the car. That just about finished her. She was exhausted from the two-day drive, and tormented still by all the unanswered questions her trip to the Northern Isles had brought up.

Once, before it had all begun, things had seemed so simple. She would take a week or two off work and have a bit of a holiday while she sorted out the house someone she had never met had very kindly, and inexplicably, left to her. She would make a leisurely drive north through Scotland, take a ferry to the islands, and then she would spend a couple of days looking over Aunt Freda's house before she arranged for it to be sold. Then she would drive home again, ready to get back to her life. That had been it — the entire plan.

Had it worked out like that? Not a bit of it. Lifting the lid on her inheritance had released an unfathomable swarm of conundrums to tease and plague her. What on earth was it all about? Why, why, why?

Just who, exactly, was this mysterious woman, Freda Nicholson? She seemed to have lived a life far from the ordinary, but what on earth had led her to bequeath her home to someone with whom she had no apparent connection?

Then there was Gregor. He had flashed into her life like a passing comet. Would she ever see him again? And even if she did, what then?

She had no idea. All she knew was that there was some thinking to be done. At least, there would be when she had recovered from the journey. Right now, all she really wanted was a hot bath and to go to bed for about ten hours. All the questions and issues could wait until tomorrow.

First, though, she needed to ring Mum, and reassure her she was all right, and back in the real world, where things were usually more understandable.

'Hello, Mum! It's me.'

'Emma! Where are you?'

She felt herself relaxing. It was so good to hear that voice again, and that good old Geordie accent that she knew so well.

'Home. I'm back home. Just got in. I was going to come over to see you, but I'm so tired it'll have to wait till tomorrow. I just wanted you to know I was back safely.'

'That's good. We were wondering. How was Orkney? Did you get everything sorted?'

'Well, not really. I'll have to go back again soon. It was all more complicated than I expected, but I'll tell you about it when I see you. I'm too tired to start now. I enjoyed the week, though. Orkney is a lovely place. Very interesting, too.'

'What about the cottage?'

'Actually, it's not a little cottage, Mum. It's a big house. But wait till tomorrow. I'll tell you all about it then.'

'All right, pet. You get yourself to bed now. We'll talk tomorrow.'

'Bye, Mum!'

She couldn't be bothered with a bath after all, she decided, so she had a quick shower instead. Then she made herself a mug of camomile tea and sat sipping it at the kitchen table. One eye caught the unpacked bag she had brought home with her. The other eye saw the pile of mail she had picked up from the hall. Her eyes moved on and she left everything alone. She couldn't be bothered with anything very much. She was so tired.

Orkney was still on her mind, though — the Mainland, Broch House, Freda, and Gregor. They were all there, in the front of her thoughts. Jennifer and Mrs McEwan, too. She had thought she had left them all behind, but she hadn't really. They were still with her, the people and the places. She could see them now. It had been such a long journey home — too long, really — but nothing had faded from memory. If anything, her memories were more vivid than ever, especially those of Gregor.

His mother and sister had combined to make him seem even more real somehow. She liked him so much, more than ever. Poor Gregor. Such sadness in his life, especially if he believed himself to be responsible for his wife's death. She wondered what had happened, and regretted not asking Jennifer for more information. Too late now, she thought with a shrug. But perhaps she would see Jennifer again. Who could tell?

Despite his loss, Gregor had done his best to overcome it. He was very busy, making his living out of what he seemed to like doing best. Freelancing had to be hard at times. Yet he had kept at it. He had also kept the memory of his wife alight. He wore her ring, as if to say she was still with him. It was how it should be, when two people who loved each other were torn apart by tragedy. She could see that.

One way or another, she felt as if she understood him so much better now. She liked him so much more, too. It was just a pity he lived so far away. They could have become friends — or even something more, perhaps, in time — but not when his life was lived there, and hers was here. Still, she might see him again when she returned to the island. She hoped so. It was something to look forward to, a straw to cling to.

Meanwhile, of course, she thought with a weary yawn, she had plenty more to think about and to investigate. Surely somebody in her family must know something about Aunt Freda? It simply defied common sense that nobody knew anything. She couldn't believe it.

Well, starting tomorrow, Sunday, she

would make a start. One thing was for sure: there was no way she could sell Broch House without first understanding more about Freda and the life she had led in the Northern Isles.

17

Sunday morning was busy. Emma put the washer on and checked the fridge to see what she was short of in the groceries department. Everything, it seemed. She grimaced. Well, she would have to manage with what she had in tins and in the freezer. She wasn't going to the supermarket on a Sunday. There were better things to do, more important things. Shopping would have to wait until after work on Monday, or even Tuesday.

Anna and Kim should be back from Greece by now — assuming they hadn't been detained by Greek waiters with offers of marriage. Or was it Turkish waiters who did that? She grinned at the thought. But would they be up by ten? Probably not. So she would leave contacting them for now, and visit Mum and Dad instead.

Before she set off, she checked the mail that had gathered during her absence. For most of it, she didn't even bother opening the envelopes. She could tell what the letters were: bank statements, credit card statements, and other communications requiring, if not actually demanding, payment. Like a lot of other things, they could wait.

The one envelope she did open enclosed a letter from the solicitor handling the English end of Aunt Freda's will. Would she phone to arrange an appointment?

Well, she would, she thought with a frown. But what did they want? Had something happened? Again, though, she could do nothing on a Sunday. So that was something else that would have to wait.

She set off for her parents' place in Gosforth. Another thing, she thought: the car needed a service. The display panel was telling her so. In another hundred miles. But that, too, could wait until Monday.

Her parents enjoyed hearing about her journey, especially the ferry crossing, which she made sound more dramatic than it actually had been.

'It's a long way north, Orkney,' Dad pronounced solemnly. 'I've had a look at the map. They'll get big seas up there.'

'And I saw them!' Emma assured him, laughing.

'A bit like it is off Whitley Bay when there's a spring tide.'

She shook her head vigorously. 'It's nothing like Whitley Bay, Dad. The North Sea there is just a millpond.'

'Oh, I don't know about that. It can get rough off the Tyne.'

She smiled sweetly, and with relief turned to Mum, who was asking about the house.

'Like I said, it's a big house. There's six bedrooms, and some lovely spacious rooms downstairs. It took me all week just to get round them all! The garden's a good size, as well.'

'Goodness! As big as that? I had no idea,' Mum said wonderingly.

That's because you know nothing at all about Aunt Freda, Emma thought with a sigh.

'Have you put it up for sale now?' Dad asked.

'No, I haven't yet. I didn't have time to sort everything out.'

'Does it need a lot of work doing to it first?' Mum asked.

Emma shook her head. 'Not really. Not at all, in fact. It's just that I want to understand it better before I take that step. I'd like to know more about Aunt Freda, as well.' She saw her parents look at each other and grimace. 'Come on, you two! Freda left me this house, and I want to know why. I also want to know what she was like, and what she was doing in Orkney all her life nearly.'

Mum shook her head. 'Oh, you don't want to go down that road, dear. It'll take forever — and for what? What good will it do? Just tell the solicitors to go ahead and sell it. Then you can get on with your own life.'

She could have told them something then of what she had learned of Aunt Freda, but she didn't. For some reason she couldn't articulate, she held back. She didn't know where to start, for one thing. Also, she sensed a lack of interest on their part. Basically, they didn't seem to want to know anything about Freda. They had asked nothing about her. It was all about the journey and the house. Nothing about Freda herself. Still, it wasn't really surprising, Emma supposed. They hadn't been in touch with Freda, and Orkney was not a place they were ever likely to go. It was just a little surprising that they weren't as puzzled as she was as to why Freda had left her the house. That sort of thing certainly didn't happen every day of the week. Hardly ever at all, in fact.

'Do you really know nothing about Aunt Freda?' she asked.

Dad shook his head. 'Not me. It's many years since I even heard the name.'

143

'And I can't remember ever seeing her,' Mum said. 'She's always just been an odd member of the family who chose to live in the back of beyond.'

'Ha!' Emma said with a chuckle. 'Orkney isn't exactly the back of beyond, Mum. It's got everything we have here — even a big Tesco!'

'Has it really? It might be worth going there sometime, then.'

'Just stop it!' Emma protested, laughing. 'It's a lovely place, and I had a wonderful week. Or ten days, or whatever it was.'

'Oh?' Mum said, giving her a suspicious look. 'Did you really? Does that mean you met someone?'

'Of course I met someone! I met a lot of people, and they were all very friendly and helpful.'

'A young man, I meant.'

'I know perfectly well what you meant, Mum. Yes, I did meet a very nice young man. He showed me around the island and helped with the house.'

'Oh? It's a long way away, though, isn't it?'

Emma began to feel a bit desperate. She knew the way her mother's mind worked, and she could see the cogs starting to turn. Orkney was a long way to go to see the grandchildren!

'It wasn't like that, Mum. Gregor is a wildlife cameraman and photographer. He's very passionate about his work, and very interesting too. What's more,' she added, 'he knew Aunt Freda. He was able to tell me a bit about her. Apparently she was something of a local celebrity.'

Mum looked even more disconcerted for a moment. Then she yawned and said, 'Sorry, dear. I didn't have a very good night last night. I'm still tired. Would you like a coffee?'

'Yes, please. Shall I make it?'

'No. You stay here and talk to your father. Keep him out of my way.'

Strange, Emma couldn't help thinking. Mum didn't seem her usual self this morning. Nor did Dad. All the things she had assumed they would want to hear about were just sailing above their heads. Perhaps they were both a bit tired.

She was about to tell Dad a bit more about the mysterious Aunt Freda when he straightened up in his chair and said, 'There'll be a lot of wildlife on Orkney, is there?'

'Oh, yes,' she told him. 'Birds and fish, and seals and things. Whales, as well,' she added vaguely. 'At least, I think so. Gregor is mainly interested in the birds, though.'

'That new series of David Attenborough's is very interesting,' Dad said. 'I'd like to go to that wildlife park in Kenya one day. But the wildebeest have a terrible time crossing that river every year, with the crocodiles waiting for them. Funny how they know exactly to the day when the herds will be coming. Uncanny, isn't it?'

So that's Orkney and Aunt Freda done with, Emma thought despondently. *They're not interested at all in* where I've been and what I've learned. I don't know why I rushed over here. I might as well have stayed in the flat and read the Sunday paper.

18

After work on Tuesday Emma met her friends, Anna and Kim, for a happy-hour pizza in a lively place in Gosforth.

'I don't want to know anything at all about Greece,' Emma announced as she arrived at the table where the others were already settled. 'Nothing at all!'

'Oh!' Kim said, with a meaningful glance at Anna. 'What does that mean, I wonder?'

'It means Emma had a terrible week in Scotland while we were sunning ourselves in Rhodes, I suppose. Sunning ourselves, swimming and drinking delicious, cheap wine,' Anna added with satisfaction.

'Not cheap!' Kim protested. 'Inexpensive is the word I would use.'

'Inexpensive-but-delicious wine then,' Anna said, accepting the correction. 'Not to mention the eligible young men hovering around us all the while.'

'Just stop it, you two!' Emma said, laughing. 'Seriously, how was it?'

'Lovely,' Kim said, 'if you really want to know.'

'Gorgeous,' Anna agreed. 'Not terribly hot, but quite warm enough for us, thank you very much.'

'The countryside is so beautiful at this time of year,' Kim said wistfully. 'Wildflowers everywhere, after the winter rain. No crowds either.'

'So what was Orkney like?' Anna asked.

'Cold and windswept, but interesting. Let's order first,' Emma suggested, waving to attract a hovering waiter. 'Then I'll tell you all about it.'

It was so good to be back with her friends. Emma began to feel happier than at any time since her return. She had missed them. What was more, she had such a lot to tell them.

'It's a big house,' she said, sipping her glass of wine. 'Six bedrooms and nice, big reception rooms. Plus a big kitchen.'

'Not a country cottage, then,' Kim said. 'That's disappointing. Oh, sorry! I didn't really mean that. It's just that I was thinking of a cosy little stone cottage with a thatched roof, and roses around the door. That sort of thing.'

Emma smiled. 'No, it's not like that. Mind you, it is built of stone, and it does have a big garden.'

'A house that big,' Anna said, 'must have a name?'

'Yes. Broch House.'

'Which means?'

'Well, Gregor told me it's an old Pictish word for fort or castle.'

'So it's a castle?'

Emma shook her head.

'Wait a minute,' Kim interjected. 'Gregor, did you say? Who, or what, is Gregor?'

'Sorry! I haven't mentioned him, have I?'

'No,' Kim said suspiciously.

'He's a very nice man I met on the ferry going over to Stromness. He's been . . . well, helping me. His mother's nice, too.'

'Helping you — how?' Kim wanted to know.

'Just a minute,' Anna said. 'You were there . . . what? A week? And you've met this man's mother already? That's going some!'

As Kim and Anna dissolved in laughter, Emma said plaintively, 'It wasn't like that. Honestly, you two!' Then she began to explain to them about Aunt Freda and the mystery surrounding her. She told them she wanted to know about this person who had so mysteriously left her a house, when she had never even met her in the whole of her life.

'You're right,' Anna said speculatively, 'it is a mystery. No wonder you wanted to find out about her.'

'What about the house?' Kim asked. 'What are you going to do with it?'

'Nothing for the moment. I want to know more about Aunt Freda before I do anything with it. The house won't come to any harm, sitting there. It's been there a couple of hundred years already.'

'And this man — Gregor? — who

you met on the ferry, is helping you?' Kim asked suspiciously. 'How is he doing that?'

'Well, he knew Freda, and he knows a bit about her. She was quite a local celebrity, apparently. She wrote books and was on the radio; gave talks. That sort of thing. Then I found some old photographs, and Gregor knew where some of them were taken. So he took me there.'

'And you've met his mother? Was she on the ferry as well?'

'Well, yes, she was actually. And please don't start giggling again! She's a very nice woman. His sister is, too.'

'His sister!' the others chorused.

'But his brother, Alastair, isn't very pleasant. In fact, he's a bit of a nuisance.'

'Well, that's something, I suppose,' Anna said philosophically. 'I'd hate to think the whole family was absolutely adorable.'

'It would destroy my faith in human nature,' Kim contributed.

'And mine,' Anna agreed. 'Now let us tell you more about Greece. Rhodes is a wonderful island that . . . '

Emma sat back with relief, prepared to listen.

Later, it was Kim who came up with a question that Gregor had also asked. 'Just how does — or did — this Aunt Freda relate to you, Emma?'

'You mean, what's the family connection?'

Kim nodded.

'Well, she's my great-aunt.'

'But your mother's actual aunt?'

Emma smiled agreement.

'Then how come the house was left to you instead of your mum? That's what I don't understand.'

'Everyone seems to want to know that, Kim,' Emma said evenly, 'including me.'

19

When she next saw her parents, Emma asked them again about Freda. Again, they had nothing to add to the very little they had previously been able to tell her.

'There are some old photographs Freda took of a POW camp in Orkney. I was wondering if she was in the army, or one of the other services. Did you ever hear anything about that?'

Mum shook her head. 'Nothing at all. Why would she have been in the army?'

'Well, because of her age, I suppose. This must have been in the war, the Second World War. A lot of women were in uniform then, weren't they?'

'I really don't know. I don't remember Gran ever talking about those times much either.' Mum shrugged and smiled. 'It was before my time, dear. I'm not that old, you know.'

'Of course you're not!' Emma laughed and shook her head. 'I never suggested you were. It is strange, though — about Aunt Freda, I mean.'

'What is?' Dad asked.

'Well, the photos of all these people in uniform, as if Aunt Freda was one of them. She was ninety-one when she died. That means she must have been twenty-two or twenty-three when the war ended. So she could have been in uniform, couldn't she?'

'A lot of women were,' Dad agreed, 'even if it was just the Land Army.'

'What was that?'

'Farm work. Women replaced the men from the farms who had gone off to war.'

'Oh, yes. I've heard of that, now I think about it. Wasn't there a film about the Land Army?'

'Probably.' Dad shrugged. Then he grinned and added, 'I find it hard to keep up with these things. Maybe you should ask your grandmother about those times. She might know more about your Aunt Freda, as well.'

'Oh, dear!' Mum said with a weary sigh. 'Please don't encourage her. Couldn't we change the subject? I'm getting awfully tired of hearing about Aunt Freda. I'm beginning to wish she'd never left you her house, Emma.'

'Sorry, Mum. At least I didn't bring you lots of old photos to wade through. Lots of new photos, either. Did I tell you about all the holiday photos of Greece I had to sit through with Anna and Kim?'

'I don't think you did, no. But I wouldn't mind seeing some of Greece, actually. What a pity you didn't go with them.'

Emma grinned. 'Oh, Orkney was far more interesting than where they went. All their photos were of the hotel pool and the local beach. I would soon have got tired of that, however welcome some warm sunshine might have been.'

They spoke then of holidays, holidays past and holidays still to come. Mum and Dad were booked to go somewhere in southern Spain once again. Mum, in particular, cherished fond memories of the place. Emma's brain glazed over as she heard about it for the umpteenth time. She was happy for them, but she had no feelings of envy at all. She was just thankful she was too old now to have to go with them.

Before she left, Emma did manage to question Mum again about Aunt Freda. 'Anna and Kim were asking me how Aunt Freda was related to me, Mum. We've been calling her Aunt Freda, but was she really a relative? The name Freda Nicholson didn't mean anything at all to me when I started getting those letters from the solicitor about her.'

'Well . . . ' Mum hesitated.

'And wasn't she your aunt, rather than mine?' Emma added.

Mum sighed, as if to say, Here we go again! 'She was Gran's sister, I believe,' she admitted reluctantly. 'So yes, she was actually your great-aunt.'

'On your mother's side,' Dad contributed helpfully, doing his best not to grin. 'My lot never had any money. Not enough to buy big houses anyway.'

'Oh, keep quiet, Dad!' Emma said, laughing. Turning back to Mum, she said, 'Gran must have talked about her, if they were sisters?'

'Well, I don't recall her doing so,' Mum said vaguely.

'And another thing,' Emma pressed. 'If she was your aunt, rather than mine, why didn't she leave her house to you, Mum, instead of to me?'

'I have no idea,' Mum said wearily. 'I have no idea at all. What's more, I don't care! I just wish you were done with the whole thing. I'm sick of hearing about it.'

'Easy!' Dad said. 'That house will be worth a lot of money, I daresay. You can't be looking a gift horse in the mouth. At least, Emma can't.'

'Gift horse?' Mum said dismissively before flouncing out of the room.

'Don't ask me,' Dad said when Emma looked at him in the hope of getting an explanation. 'I never did understand your mother's family, or your mother either, for that matter.'

'Thanks, Dad. That makes me feel a whole lot better about things,' Emma said with a grimace. 'I'd better go and see if I can calm her down.'

'That's a good idea. She's been like a cat on a hot tin roof for a few weeks now. Ever since you heard about that house, in fact.'

Emma nodded. So there was a mystery here, as well as one on Orkney, she thought wearily. A person could have too much of that sort of thing.

20

Emma found it hard to accept that her mother was so uninterested in Aunt Freda. Fair enough, she had never been to Orkney, and didn't seem to have ever met Freda, but still . . . Emma would have expected her to show more enthusiasm about this strange inheritance. Perhaps it was simply too much to comprehend if you were on the outside looking in. Dad wasn't much better either, although he did appreciate the value of the gift, in financial terms at least.

As for herself, well, she was more interested than ever. Trying to catch a glimpse of the mysterious Freda seemed to be occupying a big part of her life right now. That and Gregor, of course. They seemed to fit together somehow. There weren't many moments of the day, or the night, when thoughts of Freda,

Gregor and Orkney were far from her mind.

What a lovely man Gregor was! she thought happily once again as she did some ironing. Really, he had made that week on the island for her. If it hadn't been for him she wouldn't have seen so many of the sights Orkney had to offer. She wouldn't even have known they existed.

Skara Brae, for example. What an amazing place that Neolithic village was, and how extraordinary that neither she nor anyone else she knew back here had even heard of it. Archaeological sites were not exactly a pivotal interest for her family or her friends, of course. So perhaps their — our! — ignorance, she corrected herself, was understandable. At least Anna and Kim had both looked suitably astonished when she told them about the Neolithic village by the sea that was five thousand years old.

To think that people not so very different from us had lived there all that time ago! She liked thinking about how they might have lived back then, in their little stone-built homes under the ground, where they had found protection from the elements. Neolithic eco-homes, Gregor had called them. Built underground for warmth and shelter. A family living in each one, and each home connected to the others by underground passages, allowing people to avoid the wind and rain as much as possible.

Gregor knew so much about those times, even though he wasn't actually an archaeologist. Well, he knew so much about everything on the islands! That was what came of being born there, she supposed — or from living there a long time, like Freda.

She paused and rested the iron for a moment, thinking about Freda now. She had obviously been enthralled by Orkney's history. Perhaps that was why she had lived there most of her life. Once there, she had never wanted to leave. But why had she gone there in the first place? Emma would love to know that. In fact, she knew she wasn't going to dispose of Broch House until she did know that.

Something Dad had suggested came back to mind. Ask Gran, he had said. She might know. Know what, though? At the time, they had been talking generally about women in the armed forces in wartime. Might she know why Freda, her sister, had gone there? Perhaps Freda hadn't had a choice. Things happened to people in wartime. Ships sank, planes crashed, people lost their homes or were moved around a lot. Could Freda have been caught up in events over which she had had no control? It seemed quite possible.

For a moment, Emma wondered if Freda could have been a child evacuee, taken away from Newcastle, say, to a safer place. It was an idea she soon dismissed. That didn't work. For a start, with Scapa Flow the home of the Home Fleet, or whatever it was called, Mainland probably hadn't been all that safe. Plus, it was a long way to go. Plus again — the clincher — Freda would no longer have been a schoolgirl when the war broke out. She would have been . . . what? A quick calculation told Emma that Freda would have been sixteen or seventeen in 1939. She might still have been at school, but she didn't think sixth-formers had been evacuated from the cities. It had been much younger children. Still, that was something she could research on the internet, just in case she was mistaken. There were bound to be websites with information about things like that.

In the meantime, perhaps at the weekend, she might visit Gran to see what she could recall about her sister in those days. Not much, probably, Emma thought with a sigh. Poor Gran. Her memory wasn't great now. She would have to try to catch her on one of her good days.

As she was hanging up her freshly ironed blouses and sweaters, the phone rang.

'How's Geordieland?' a voice asked

in the accent she was coming to know so well.

'Gregor!' she cried with delight. 'I was just wondering about you. What are you up to? Geordieland is fine, by the way, thank you very much.'

'That's good. I've been pretty busy lately myself. The bird migrations are well under way. So there's plenty for me to be filming.'

'Are the birds coming in or going out?'

'They're the inward migrants, the birds that come here to nest and breed, or to rest before heading further south. The residents are at it as well of course, in places like the Brough of Birsay. Remember the cliffs there?'

'Of course. It was wonderful.'

'Well, those cliffs are gradually being covered by nesting birds.'

It was lovely to hear him, and to hear him talking so enthusiastically about his work. She was quite envious. Most of all, though, she was quietly thrilled that he had made the effort to get in touch with her. Perhaps it meant something?

'Any progress with Freda?' Gregor asked, calling a halt to the bird conversation.

'No, not really. Mum and Dad still say they know nothing about her. Anyway, I'm going to visit my gran at the weekend, to see what she can tell me about her sister, Freda.'

'She's still alive? She must be a good age.'

'Yes, she's still with us, happily. She lives in a residential home in Newcastle. Her memory isn't very good these days, unfortunately, and she sleeps a lot. I'll just have to hope I can catch her on one of her good days.'

'She ought to be able to tell you something about her own sister, don't you think?'

'I hope so.'

'Well, good luck with that. It could be interesting.' Gregor paused and then said, 'That reminds me of something I was thinking about. You remember those old photos of Freda's?'

'With the POWs?'

'Yes. I was wondering if Freda herself was in uniform at the time. Like I said before, I wouldn't have thought she would have been allowed anywhere near a POW camp if she was just a civilian.'

'I see what you mean. I was thinking about that time myself, but from a different perspective. A lot of women in those days seem to have been in the Land Army, or something similar, and Freda would have been the right age to be in uniform amongst them.'

'How old was she?'

'Ninety-one when she died. So when war broke out she'd have been sixteen or seventeen.'

'A bit young, perhaps, to have been in uniform in those days.'

'Yes, but you have to remember that by the time the war finished she would have been twenty-two or twenty-three.'

'That's true. Well, I think you've got some good questions there to put to your grandmother, haven't you? She ought to be able to answer some of them.'

'I hope so.'

'Something else I wanted to ask you, Emma. When do you think you might be coming back here? Any idea?'

Her heart jumped, and possibly missed a beat or two. 'Soon, I hope.'

'I hope so, too,' he said gravely. 'Make sure you let me know in good time. I don't want to be away when you come.'

She promised she would. After the phone call ended, she sat and thought about the implications, and what it all meant. For the moment, at least, she wasn't even thinking about Aunt Freda. She was thinking only of Gregor.

I'll go back soon, she promised herself. *I will.*

Despite the warnings she'd received from Gregor's sister, as well as his brother, she knew she couldn't wait to see him again.

21

On Saturday afternoon Emma visited her grandmother, who lived in a residential home in Gosforth. It was a pleasant, friendly place, and Gran seemed happy there. As she had once confided to Emma, she didn't have to bother with cooking and cleaning anymore. That had all become too much for her towards the end of her ninth decade, and there had been much relief in the family when somewhere nice had been found for her not far from where Emma's parents lived.

It was quiet and relaxed that afternoon, and Gran was pleased that she had a visitor. Emma tried to get to see her every couple of weeks, but that hadn't been happening lately, as she felt she needed to explain.

'I've been on holiday, Gran. And there's just been one thing after another to see to and sort out since then. Anyway, how are you?'

The old lady smiled from the depths of the chair she occupied in the residents' lounge and said, 'Well, I haven't been playing football for a while, or anything like that, but I'm quite well, thank you, Emma.'

'That's good,' Emma said with a chuckle. 'You're still in good form, I see, Gran! It's lovely to see you again.'

Smiling still, the old lady said, 'Have you just come from work?'

'No, not today, Gran. It's Saturday today.'

'Oh, is it? I didn't know. They don't tell you anything in here, you know.'

'They'll be too busy, I expect.'

'Yes, that's right. So where did you go on your holiday?'

Emma was relieved. She knew by now that she had come on a day when Gran was feeling well enough to talk to her. That wasn't always the case, sadly.

'Well, I was going to go to Greece, with my friends, Kim and Anna, but something happened and I had to change my plans.' She started to tell her about inheriting Great-aunt Freda's house in Orkney. But it wasn't long before she realised Gran had switched off.

'Gran, you know about Aunt Freda passing away, don't you?'

'Do I? Yes, I suppose I do. Somebody must have told me. Was it your mother, or the doctor? I can't remember now.'

'I'm sure Mum will have told you. Anyway, that was a while ago. What I learned just a couple of months ago was that she had left me her house in her will.'

'Who? Freda?'

'Yes. It's in Orkney, where I went recently to see it.'

Gran shook her head. 'I didn't know Freda had a house. She never had a lot of money, you know.'

'Well, she did. It's a lovely big house, too. I'll have to sell it, I suppose. But before I do, I want to know more about Freda. I also want to know why she left the house to me. Nobody else seems to have a clue, and I hoped you might be able to help me find out.'

'Me? Oh, no! I know nothing about it.'

'Not about the house, perhaps, but you do know something about Freda, don't you?'

'No, nothing,' Gran said stubbornly.

'Gran, she was your sister! You must know something. At least you know what she was like when you were both young.'

The old lady shook her head, and a crafty look came into her eyes. 'I don't remember now. It's such a long time since I last saw her. What did you say her name was again? Freda?'

Emma could have wept with frustration. Instead, she made herself calm down and look for ways of distracting the old lady, who she felt knew more than she was admitting. She focused on a vase of flowers. 'Those are lovely roses, Gran.'

'The ones on the window sill? Yes,

they are nice. Mrs Cummings, from my church, brought them the other day. They're a beautiful pink, aren't they?'

'They are,' Emma agreed shamelessly. 'Absolutely lovely. I wish I'd thought to bring you some flowers, Gran. But I was in such a hurry I forgot.' She stood up and crossed the room to sniff the roses. 'They have a nice scent, too. So many flowers you see in the shops these days smell of nothing at all.'

'I do agree,' said Gran, who seemed to be much happier with this topic of conversation. 'Do you know, I've said to more than one person not to bring me any more flowers from supermarkets or petrol stations, because they're no better than artificial flowers.'

Emma laughed. *Not much wrong with your short-term memory, Gran dear, is there?* she thought. *So there can't be much wrong with your long-term memory either. In fact, you're just like Mum! Seemingly remembering only what you want to remember.* She wondered if either of them could have reason to forget Freda. It was almost as if they had signed a pact to obliterate her from history. Was she such a terrible person? It hadn't sounded like it, from what Emma had learnt on Orkney.

'I was just wondering, Gran. In the war, were you and Freda in the army, or the Land Army, or something? Were you both in uniform, like so many women your age?'

Gran chuckled as she thought about that one. 'In the war? Oh yes — I was, anyway. I was in the Land Army, working on a farm in Cumbria. We had a lovely time in the spring, when the lambs were born. It was wonderful to see them racing around the fields. Somewhere,' she added, 'there are photos from those days. Perhaps your mother has them? I've lost track of all sorts of things since I've been in here. I don't have any of my possessions with me, you know. It's awful.'

'I'm sorry about that, Gran. I'll have to see if I can do anything about it. Was

Freda with you?'

'Freda?'

'Your sister. Was she in the Land Army with you?'

'Oh, no! Not Freda. She was far too . . . intelligent for that sort of thing. At school she was good at foreign languages, you know. I remember that.' The old lady paused for thought, and then added, 'She wouldn't have enjoyed watching lambs and harvesting potatoes — not Freda. Oh, no! Freda was in that other lot.'

'What other lot, Gran?'

'Something else. I can't recall now what it was.' The smile left her face, which took on the same obstinate look Emma had seen earlier.

'You don't know what service she was in, exactly, but it was in uniform, was it?'

'I don't remember. You shouldn't ask me things I can't remember. I'm nearly ninety, you know. I don't have to remember everything now. It can't be expected.'

'No, of course not, Gran. You're quite

right. I'm not trying to trick you. I just wanted to learn something about Freda. After all, she's left me her house in Orkney. I ought to find out something about her before I sell it, don't you think?'

'Well, it's no good asking me — or your mother either,' Gran said firmly.

'I think I've realised that already,' Emma said wearily, wondering if she was being terribly mean in pursuing the matter.

'You'll have to ask somebody else,' Gran said even more firmly. 'But I don't know who,' she added with apparent satisfaction. 'I'm probably the only one left from those days.'

Those days? What days? Wartime, did she mean? Well, she must be very nearly right about that, Emma thought sadly. 'Oh, it doesn't really matter, Gran! I didn't want to bother you. It's not that important.'

'That's good,' Gran said. Then she seemed to brighten up in relief. 'Next time you come, Emma, please bring me some more roses. I won't mind if they're only from the supermarket. I realise you won't have a lot of money.'

'All right, Gran. I will.'

You scheming old thing! Emma thought with amusement. *There I was feeling sorry for you, because I seemed to be badgering you. But you were just playing with me, weren't you? I wonder what it is you don't want me to know.*

Soon afterwards Emma left, knowing she had learned something despite the old lady's determination to tell her absolutely nothing at all. In fact she had learned quite a lot, she realised when she thought about it.

22

Talking to Gran, and getting such a limited response, spurred Emma on to think more about what the war-time world must have been like for young women. How did the likes of Gran and her sister fit into that world? The more she thought about it, the more Emma realised how very little she knew of those times. How did women end up in uniform, for example, and which uniform?

There was only one thing to do. She set an evening aside and got onto her computer to do some research. Some of the answers she wanted were easy to find. There was far more information available online than she would have thought possible.

She found that, after a slow start, an Act of Parliament in December 1941 provided for the conscription of young women into national service. At first it applied to childless widows and single women between the ages of twenty and thirty. Later, the age range became nineteen to forty-three. The country simply didn't have enough men to do what was required by the armed forces and the wartime economy. The nation's women had to be mobilised.

Once women were signed up, they could choose between civilian work — in industry or on the land — or the armed forces. Eighty thousand women entered the Land Army, which was a civilian force, and thousands of others worked in forestry. Soon a third of the jobs even in industry were filled by women.

It was a bit of an eye-opener. Emma hadn't realised the scale of female participation in the workforce, or the contribution women made to the economy and the war effort back in those days. She had believed it had all started with the feminists in the 1960s and 70s, not with World War II.

Interesting as all this was, however, she focused on women who had entered the various uniform services. The information she found wasn't easy to digest. There was such a wealth of it, for one thing, and the possibilities seemed endless. How on earth had women chosen what to do, faced with such a baffling array of possibilities? Not all the uniform services were military, either. The Land Army was one civilian force with a uniform. Another was FANY, the First Aid Nursing Yeomanry. There were others.

It was perfectly possible that Freda had been in a civilian force, but Emma decided to assume that had not been the case. Apart from Gran's reluctant admission that Freda had not been in the Land Army, like her, there were all the old photographs to suggest she had been closer to the military. As Gregor had suggested, it seemed unlikely that a civilian would have been allowed access to a POW camp.

So where did that leave her? Well, the

options were still plentiful. The army, navy and air force had all had women's equivalents: the ATS, WRNS, WAAF. It didn't stop there either. There was all sorts of smaller specialist forces. It was bewildering and baffling. Emma's eyes began to glaze over at the proliferation of capital letters, and her brain ground to a standstill.

She switched off, yawned and got herself a mug of hot chocolate. She needed to do more thinking, and for that she needed some fortification.

With a further surge of energy, she discovered that the ATS, the Auxiliary Territorial Service, seemed to have been the biggest of the military organisations for women. Essentially, that was the female side of the army. Statistically, the odds were that Freda had been in the ATS. But would a young woman volunteering to join the army have been posted to remote Orkney?

★   ★   ★

She put that question to Gregor when she next spoke to him on the phone.

He chuckled. 'You still make the mistake of thinking Orkney is on the edge of the world, don't you?'

'Well ... I don't mean to be disparaging, Gregor, but it is, isn't it?'

'Have you learned nothing from everything I've been telling you? Skara Brae, where I took you that day, was here a couple of thousand years before Stonehenge was built.'

'Well, yes, but ...'

'Orkney has always been on important pathways. In ancient times people didn't travel over land. They travelled by sea and river. How long do you think it would have taken to get from London to Stromness over land before there were any railways, roads or aircraft? And that's assuming nobody killed you en route!'

'Mm, I see what you mean. But 1940 was not ancient times, was it?'

'Indeed not. Think about Scapa Flow. Didn't I tell you that was where the Home Fleet was based?'

'Yes, I believe you did, Professor — now that you mention it.'

'Watch it! So with umpteen battleships, cruisers, destroyers, and whatever else they had in those days, stationed in Scapa Flow, how many people would they have needed to support them, do you suppose?'

'A lot?' she said tentatively.

'A lot, a very lot. A hundred thousand people were shipped into Orkney to support the Home Fleet and everything else going on here. Orkney was critical, as well, to the North Atlantic convoys that brought the food the country needed.'

Emma shook her head. She hadn't thought of any of this. 'And a lot of the hundred thousand people would have been in the armed forces?'

'Armed forces, War Ministry, civil servants . . . '

'Including women in the ATS, the WRNS and ATS?'

'Absolutely — whatever they are, or were!'

She laughed. 'Oh, I'm ahead of you there, am I? That's good. I've been doing some research into the wartime conscription of women. It's proved to be very interesting.'

'And it sounds like time well spent. But have you found anything more on Freda?'

'Not yet. I've got some ideas I'm going to follow up, though, now you've set me right on the importance of Orkney. I just couldn't see how Freda could have ended up there, but you've given me something to think about. Perhaps she had no choice?'

'I think that's very likely. In wartime people were probably told where to go, and what to do when they got there. By the way, my own guess would be that Freda was more likely to have been in the navy than the army. After all, Scapa Flow was a naval base.'

'That's true,' Emma said thoughtfully. 'I hadn't looked at it like that.'

'It's worth thinking about.'

She absorbed that suggestion, and

then changed the subject. 'By the way, I'm coming back in a fortnight's time. I've arranged with my boss to have some more time off work.'

'Really? Oh, that's great news. I shall look forward to that.'

And so shall I, Emma thought with a smile and a lift of her heart.

23

When Emma met Anna and Kim next, they complained that she had been neglecting them.

'How can you say that?' she complained right back. 'Here I am, sitting here with you both, drinking wine, eating pizza, enjoying myself.'

'Now you're a property owner,' Anna said with a haughty sniff, 'we're not good enough for you, are we?'

'I don't feel like a property owner. I still live in my rented one-bedroom flat.'

'Just as an experiment. To see how most of us live.'

It was impossible to keep a straight face. Laughing out loud, Emma said, 'I don't know why I bother with you two!'

'Actually,' Kim intervened thoughtfully, 'I don't think it has anything to do with a house. I think it's all to do with that man she found on Orkney. What was his name again?'

'Gregory, wasn't it?' Anna said helpfully.

'Gregor, actually,' Emma corrected her automatically. Then she eyed Kim with a whimsical look and added, 'You're not totally wrong, you know. He's a lovely man. And I'm pleased to say he phones me quite often.'

'Oh!' they chorused, wide-eyed. 'He phones her!'

Emma shrugged. 'Unfortunately, it's not what you think. He phones me in the interest of research. We're both trying to find out more about this aunt who left me her house, which is far more difficult than you two might think.'

'So you said,' Anna responded with a smile, relenting. 'Has no one in your family been able to help?'

'Not much. Mum and Dad don't seem to know anything about Aunt Freda. The only other person who ought to know something is Gran,

Freda's sister, but she can't remember much.'

'Why doesn't your mum know anything?' Anna asked with a frown.

'I don't know,' Emma said, shaking her head. 'She seems to have barely heard of Freda. Probably it's because she lived so far away on Orkney nearly all her life.'

'Have you worked out how she got there in the first place?' Kim asked.

'Not yet. We — that's me and Gregor — are wondering if she was conscripted and sent there by the army, or the navy, when the war started. But we haven't found any proof. We're still working on it.'

'Which war was that?' Anna asked thoughtfully.

'World War Two, of course.'

'Not the First World War?'

'No, of course not. Freda wasn't that old. Anyway, I'm going back up there in a couple of weeks. Apart from all this wondering about Freda, I still have to do something with the house. Sell it, I suppose, although I'm not really ready to do that just yet.'

'Going back to basics,' Kim said, 'why can't you and Gregor be romantically inclined? Why does it have to be only about research about Freda?'

'I wondered when you'd get back to that!' Emma said with a grin. 'Gregor's a lovely man, but he's damaged goods, sadly. His sister warned me that he isn't interested in women generally, and he doesn't seem to be interested in me particularly. Not that way, at least.'

Kim frowned. 'Oh? Is he . . . you know? Gay?'

'No, I'm sure he isn't.'

'Well, then?'

Emma sighed. 'I don't know much about it, but it's very sad. Apparently he was married and lost his wife in a bad road accident somewhere in Africa.'

'Africa?'

'He's a wildlife cameraman — didn't I tell you? — and took her on safari, or something, with him. His sister says he blames himself for taking her, but he

189

didn't really have a choice.' With a shrug, Emma added, 'That's all I really know.'

'How sad,' Kim said. 'So he remains faithful to her memory?'

Emma nodded. 'I do like him, though.'

'So do I,' Anna said. 'I like him already. He sounds very romantic.'

Emma stared at her a moment, and then shook her head and began to laugh.

'What?' Anna protested. 'Why can't I like him? Just because I've never met him doesn't mean — '

'Will you tell her,' Kim asked Emma abruptly, 'or do you want me to do it?'

★   ★   ★

Back at the flat that evening, Emma fired up her laptop again and spent some more time pursuing Freda. Now she knew a little about how it was in wartime, she could find her way around the subject a bit more easily. Already she had come across websites that offered the possibility of tracing the military service records of individual people. One commercial site offered access to the records of seven million people, although they were spread over a great many wars. Another claimed to have fifty million records, spanning the centuries, as well as the nations. It didn't stop there either. She wondered who on earth had done the work to put all this online.

She focused on websites run by the National Archives, a branch of government, which were official and she felt would be reliable. Unfortunately, she soon realised she had hit the buffers, at least in the short term. Her task would have been easier if Freda had been alive during the First World War. Then she could have looked for her online. World War II personnel records were a different matter. They were held still by the Ministry of Defence, and amazingly, after all this time, were still too recent to be made available online for reasons of confidentiality.

It was possible to obtain certain limited information about a person's military service record in the 1939–45 period if you were next of kin, or even just for research purposes, but for that you needed to apply to the Ministry of Defence. Emma made some notes on what was required, but then rather lost interest when she read that processing the application could take many months.

She grimaced with disappointment and frustration. She needed to know now, or at least very soon. It wouldn't be possible to defer a decision about the house all that time. Still, she supposed it might be worth making an application anyway, just to see what happened.

Late as it was, she wasn't really tired enough to sleep. She decided to do a little more searching. Particularly interesting were the archives compiled by the BBC and other organisations containing the personal stories of women who had been contemporaries of Freda's. It was truly astonishing. Young women had been uprooted from their homes and lives to be sent all over the place, and in all sorts of uniforms. Some — plenty — had disagreeable experiences, even if they were not manning front-line trenches. But they were young, and the times were exciting. For many of the women it was the time of their life, at least in retrospect.

There were thousands of stories reported in brief in the online archives. Far too many to read through in one lifetime, but they were there, on record, as testimony to a time now long gone, like most of the participants.

Scanning the titles of the contributions to one website, Emma noticed a story recorded by a Wren who had been sent to Orkney to serve on HMS Tern. It stuck in her mind, partly because it was about Orkney, and partly because she knew Gregor was interested in terns. She would tell him about that one, and ask him about HMS Tern.

24

'I've brought you some flowers, Gran — and they're not from the supermarket either! These are from a proper florist.' *And they cost an arm and a leg,* she thought to herself with a wry smile.

'Oh, I do love roses! They're beautiful, dear. Thank you so much.'

Emma found a vase, filled it with water, and then sat and watched while Gran arranged the roses in it to her satisfaction.

'Red roses,' Gran said. 'Even nicer than pink. But you shouldn't have gone to all that trouble, Emma.'

'It's no trouble, Gran. Don't be silly. I just wish there was more I could do for you.'

'Nonsense! You all do quite enough.'

Gran seemed to be feeling well and happy today, Emma thought. She was pleased about that. She also felt a little guilty, because she hoped to squeeze a little more information out of her. The roses were not exactly a bribe — she would have brought them anyway — but if they helped, then so be it.

'I'm going back up to Orkney at the weekend, Gran.'

'Are you really?'

'Yes. So I wanted to see you again before I go. I'll be away a fortnight this time, and I don't want you worrying about why I've not been to see you.'

The old lady chuckled. 'You deserve a break, but Orkney again? It's not long since you were there, is it?'

'No. Just a few weeks.'

'You don't have a young man there, do you?'

'Gran! What would I be doing with a young man there, when I work and live here? No, unfortunately, it's not about a young man. It's mostly about Aunt Freda's house. I need to do something about it.'

'Oh?'

'I did tell you about how she had left

it to me, didn't I?'

'Yes. That was kind of her.'

'Well, I'm sure she was a kind person.'

'Yes, she was — sometimes. She wasn't always, though. I remember she was very rude about how I looked in my uniform. I was in the Land Army, you know?'

'And Freda wasn't, as I recall you telling me last time I was here.'

'Oh, no! Freda was far too good for that. She was a clever girl, a lot cleverer than me.'

Emma held her breath. This was gold, pure gold! Somehow she had struck a rich vein. If she moved on gently, not pressing too hard . . . 'You said Freda was in 'that other lot'. What kind of uniform did she have?'

'Oh, hers was very smart, I admit it. I liked mine well enough, but Freda's was a different class, much better. The little hat she wore just finished it off nicely.'

'Definitely not the Land Army, then?'

'Oh, no! Freda always wanted to join the navy, and that's just what she did.'

'And got herself posted to Orkney?'

There was no response to that. Emma waited, but there was nothing more.

Gran finished with the flowers and sat back down, smiling. 'They're lovely, don't you think?'

'I do. You're an expert at flower arranging, aren't you?'

'Oh, I wouldn't say that. But in the WI you learn such a lot about that sort of thing.'

'So off Freda went to Orkney, in her smart new uniform,' Emma said, deciding to push her luck a little further.

Gran nodded. 'Yes. She was very happy there, we believed. Of course it all changed with the baby, didn't it?'

'Baby? Gran, did Freda have a baby?'

The smile, and the light, seemed to vanish from Gran's face in an instant. 'Oh, dear!' she said, putting a hand to her head. 'I don't feel at all well.'

Emma jumped up and rang for a

carer, alarmed that she had precipitated some crisis with her questions. Fortunately, it was soon established that all was well. A little attention and a cup of sweet tea, together with a paracetamol, seemed to do the trick. Emma relaxed as the old lady revived. In time, she even resumed her questioning.

'What were you saying about Freda and the baby?' she asked casually.

Gran stared at her for a moment with a flash of irritation. Then, sounding and looking quite mystified, she said, 'What baby? I don't know anything about anybody having a baby, not in our family.'

Oh dear, Emma thought with frustration. *I'm not sure, but I think I've been out-manoeuvred — again!*

* * *

That evening she told her parents about her visit to Gran. 'She remembered a bit more about Aunt Freda. She said she was in the navy. Is that possible?'

'I shouldn't think so,' Mum said firmly. 'Oh, Emma! I do wish you'd just forget all this nonsense about Aunt Freda, for goodness sake! Just sell the house and get on with your own life.'

'I don't know why you think it's nonsense, Mum, because it isn't. Not to me. It's important to me to know why Freda left me her house. I can't just sell the thing without knowing anything about her. Anyway, I enjoyed my time on Orkney, which is why I'm going back again. I met some interesting people and saw some interesting places.'

'You don't have to go all that way to find interesting people and places. There's plenty in Spain, for a start. Take where we're going in the summer.'

Emma giggled and looked at her father, who started to chuckle.

'What?' Mum said irritably. 'What are you both laughing at?'

'Mum, where you and Dad are going in the summer is three or four times as far away as Orkney — and you'll need a plane to get there!'

'That's all I need,' Mum snapped. 'A geography lesson from my daughter!' She left to sort out something in the kitchen, she said, and perhaps to recover her dignity.

Emma asked her dad, 'Why is Mum so set against me going back to Orkney?'

'I have no idea. Do you think she is, really?'

'Yes, I do. Whenever I mention the place, she always changes the subject or makes her lack of interest very clear. I don't understand it. Gran isn't much different either. Mind you, Gran was unusually forthcoming this time. As well as telling me Freda was in the navy, she said she had a baby at some point. But then she clammed up again. I couldn't get anything more out of her.'

'A baby? Well, I've never heard anything about that. Not that I've ever heard much at all about Freda anyway. I'll let you know if I find out anything more from your mother.' He thought about it, frowned and added, 'Interesting that Gran told you Freda was in the navy. I'd never heard that before either. The WRNS, it will have been. Freda a Wren, eh? That'll be how she ended up in Orkney. She'll have been posted there.'

'Yes, that's what I'm thinking.'

'She probably wasn't very happy about it either. The back of beyond? She'd have wanted to be in London, I expect, like all the rest of them.'

'Well, she stayed there, didn't she? She must have liked it. Anyway, Dad. Back of beyond? That's not what Gregor calls it. He says it's always been busy, and on the main routes to . . . well, everywhere, basically.'

'Gregor? Who's that? I haven't heard that name before. Well, not since Gregor Townsend stopped playing rugby for Scotland.'

'Just a friend, Dad. A man I met on the ferry. He's been helping me with the house and things.'

'Oh, aye?' Dad said with a knowing

201

smile. 'No wonder you're keen to go back there.'

'It's not what you think, Dad. Unfortunately,' she added with a wry smile.

★　★　★

When Emma rang Gregor next, a day or two before she was setting off, she told him what she had learned.

'So she really was in the Wrens? That's interesting.'

'Very. It gets us a little bit closer to Freda. I've made a request to the Ministry of Defence to see if I can obtain her service record, but I'm likely to have a long wait, unfortunately. Months, apparently, as they work their way down the list of enquiries. In the meantime, I've thought of something else. I read a little piece in an online archive about a woman who joined the WRNS and was posted to Orkney. She was sent to HMS Tern. I realise there'll have been lots of ships there at the time, but I just wonder if Freda could have been sent to that one as well. Do you think it's possible to check what it was like? Is there a museum that might have stuff like that?'

'Yes — the Orkney Museum in Kirkwall is very good. I'll see what I can find out there. But you'll be here soon, won't you?'

'Yes. On Monday, I hope.'

'I'm looking forward to that, Emma,' he said quietly.

'Me, too,' she assured him.

Afterwards, she wondered if she had been too eager to respond. She didn't want to frighten him away. *No,* she thought, *it'll be all right. He'll just assume that, like him, I was thinking of the house and Freda. I hope so, anyway,* she concluded with a resigned shrug. Some things were out of her hands.

25

Emma liked driving. She was good at it and had always enjoyed being behind the wheel of a moving vehicle. So, although she could have made her way back to Orkney by train and plane, she much preferred to drive up to Thurso and then take the ferry across to Stromness again. Once there, she would need a car to get around the island anyway, and hiring one would add to the cost.

It took her all day to get to Thurso, but that wasn't a hardship. She had been before, and knew the route. Once she was past Edinburgh, it was easy driving through beautiful countryside and along the spectacular east coast of Scotland. Now it was May, the journey was even more enjoyable than it had been the first time she made it.

Most of the way, she was relaxed and had plenty of time to think. What to do with Broch House had to be top of her agenda. She knew that she had been procrastinating too long about putting it on the market. An empty house could fall apart, even be vandalised, if there was no one there to care for it. She didn't want that to happen. She had better get on and make arrangements to sell it now summer was just about here.

And yet, was she really ready to do that? It still seemed premature somehow to put the house on the market without knowing more about Freda. She grimaced. She did want to be sure she was doing the right thing, and how could she when she still knew so little?

Mind you, she thought with a wry smile, *I know a lot more than I did a couple of months ago. Freda has become a real person to me. So I must carry on a bit longer. I'm determined to learn a lot more about her, now I've made a start. Then we'll see about the house. It can wait a little bit longer.*

Then there was Gregor. He was real enough, and in her thoughts, too. But she didn't really want to think too much about Gregor. She would see him soon enough. Perhaps then she would have a better idea of where she stood with him.

If he was even slightly interested in her, then she might be more interested in him. But if, as his sister had suggested, he was a one-woman guy, and loyal for life to his late wife, she would accept that. Even if only as a friend, she wanted to know Gregor, and to see him. It was just that she was determined not to put too many eggs in one basket. She had to leave herself with freedom to manoeuvre, if it came to that, without untold emotional damage to herself. She wasn't some besotted teenager, for heaven's sake!

★　★　★

The sun was still shining when she reached Thurso and booked into the B&B where she had stayed on her previous visit.

'Have you come all the way in one go?' the woman who ran the place asked.

Emma nodded.

'You've had a long day.'

'A good one, though. I enjoyed the drive.'

'Good for you.' The woman smiled and added, 'I always think this is the best time of year to be travelling in the north. Are you booked on the ferry for tomorrow?'

'I am. I'm afraid it'll be an early start.'

'Breakfast at seven OK?'

'If it's not inconvenient.'

'Not at all. We're used to people travelling on the ferry. I'll let you get away to your room now. You'll no doubt be wanting an early night?'

Emma nodded gratefully. She was looking forward to a good night's sleep.

★ ★ ★

She was awake and on her way early. The ferry to Stromness sailed exactly on time as well. *Two hours*, she thought with a glance at her watch. *Two hours, and I'll be there. I'll see Gregor again. And everything else, of course*, she cautioned herself, impatient that she had let down her guard for a moment.

The sea was flat that day, not at all like it had been when she last saw it. The sun was shining, too, and the wind was no more than a gentle breeze. Summer, she thought happily. Even here!

She watched Hoy loom into view, and remembered what Gregor had told her about the island. Somehow it looked less fierce this time, with the sun shining nicely on dry rock and a gentle sea lapping lazily at the base of the cliffs.

After a coffee in the lounge, she returned to the deck in time to see Stromness come into view. How familiar it looked, she thought, as she watched the first houses appear, and then the first of the slipways and the boatyards. She shivered with expectation. She was here!

She might be here, but Gregor wasn't here to meet her. As she drove cautiously off the ferry, she looked in vain for him. There were only a few people waiting and watching, and she couldn't see Gregor amongst them. She crossed the open space on the quayside, looking around eagerly, but still she couldn't see him. She pulled to one side, out of the flow of traffic emerging from the ship, and waited, wondering what to do.

No Gregor, but suddenly there was a woman walking briskly towards her car and waving energetically. 'Remember me?' the woman asked when Emma lowered her window.

'Oh, Jennifer! Sorry. I didn't recognise you for a moment.'

'Gregor asked me to meet you. Can I get in?'

'Of course.'

Jennifer got into the passenger seat and smiled at her. 'Good to see you again. How are you, Emma?'

'I'm fine, thank you. You?'

'Stressed, run off my feet and . . . I'm fine, too. But the kids have been driving me crazy lately. And I need more sleep!'

Emma laughed. She was pleased to see Jennifer, but a little puzzled, too. 'I was expecting to see — '

'I know, I know! Gregor told me. But something came up to do with his work, unfortunately. He couldn't be here, and asked me to meet you instead. Do you fancy a coffee, by the way? There's a nice little café just across the road. I can tell you all about it there.'

Emma was disappointed not to see Gregor. She had been looking forward so much to seeing him again, but at least he had sent Jennifer to explain. That was something. He hadn't just stood her up or forgotten about her. Anyway, she liked Jennifer, and found her good company.

'So these stupid chicks are finally about to emerge from their egg shells,'

Jennifer told her once they were settled in the café, 'and poor Gregor has had to be there day and night until they do. I told him I agree with Mother. I said it's time he got a proper job. At his age, he should be going to work every day at a sensible time, like nine o'clock in the morning, and getting home in time for supper.'

Emma laughed. 'You didn't, did you?'

'Not really, no. At least, I didn't mean it.'

'I think he has a wonderful career already.'

'Yes, of course he has. But it's hard work, and inconvenient at times. Oh, good! Here's our coffee.'

Jennifer obviously knew the waitress who had appeared at their table with a laden tray. Emma listened to their friendly exchanges about everyday life and family affairs. Probably, she thought, everyone knew everyone else on this island. It wasn't like living in a big city.

'Luckily for Gregor,' Jennifer resumed

when the waitress had left them to it, 'I could be here in time to meet you. I packed the kids off to school and raced across from Kirkwall.'

'It was very good of you, Jennifer, but you didn't really need to do it. I know where I'm going, and where everything is.'

'Nonsense. Somebody had to meet you. Anyway, it's good for me to get out of the house. I needed a change of scene.'

'We all need that from time to time. So you have a family?'

'Yes. Husband Ken, and two children.'

Jennifer went on to say that both Elizabeth and Thomas were in school now, which made domestic life a little easier for her. Ken worked on an oil platform off Shetland. He was home and away alternate months. Emma found herself wondering if Jennifer would have preferred a more conventional working life for her husband, as well as for her brother. She seemed to be everybody's go-to person, and probably could do with some help at times.

'The coffee's good,' she remarked when she had heard enough of domestic matters.

'Mm. Not bad, is it? Alison wouldn't dare serve it otherwise. No one would come back!'

Emma laughed. She did like Jennifer. She was so light-hearted and friendly, a younger version of her mother perhaps.

'Gregor told me that you both have been trying to find out more about your aunt. It's strange that you know so little about her, when she was quite a celebrity here in Orkney.'

'I know. You're right, it's strange. Before I came here the first time, I knew nothing at all about her. Mum and Dad didn't seem to either. My gran does, or should, but her memory isn't very good these days. Inheriting the house was a real shock. The news came without any warning at all. I knew there was an Aunt Freda in the family — my grandmother's sister, as it turns out

— but nothing else. I didn't know anything about Orkney either. So I've wanted to find out a bit more about Freda and Orkney before I decide what to do about Broch House.'

'Do you think you'll sell it to Alastair?'

'Your brother?' She shrugged. 'I really have no idea. At the moment I'm still concentrating on finding out more about Freda.'

Jennifer nodded. 'Gregor told me that, as well. I think you're doing the right thing, by the way. I respect you for it. Good luck.'

'Thank you,' Emma said with some surprise. 'My mother thinks I'm mad.'

'All mothers are mad, aren't they? To their daughters, at least.'

The two of them laughed at that.

'By the way,' Jennifer said, 'Gregor told me to tell you he'll catch up with you later in Birsay.'

'OK. Thank you.'

'You two seem to be getting on well together.'

'Yes, we are. He's a nice man.'

'He thinks a lot of you, you know?' Jennifer said gently. 'I'm surprised, but I'm pleased as well. Since Maggie died I've always thought he wanted to spend the rest of his life alone. Now I'm not so sure. Oh, dear!' she added, wincing. 'I'm sorry. I didn't mean to be so presumptuous. I have no idea how you feel.'

'It's all right,' Emma assured her. 'Really. You're his sister. It's very natural for a sister to be concerned about her brother. I like Gregor a lot, but we're just friends, as I told you the last time we spoke. Anyway, it's early days yet. Who knows what will happen?'

'Who, indeed? Well, good luck with everything. I'd better be away now. Lots to do. Perhaps I'll see you again while you're here?'

'I hope so, Jennifer.'

'Let me know if Ally is a nuisance again. I'll come and sort him out!'

Emma laughed and waved her goodbye.

26

Gregor turned up at the guesthouse where Emma was staying later that afternoon, as promised. Neil, the co-owner, tapped on the door of Emma's room to say she had a guest downstairs.

'Thanks Neil! I'll be down in a moment.'

She took a quick look at herself in the mirror, ran a brush over her hair a couple of times, and practised a smile that she hoped wouldn't look nervous. *Right!* she thought. *I'm as ready as I'll ever be.*

Gregor was standing at the window of the residents' lounge, gazing pensively out at the gardens.

'Gregor!'

He spun round and gave her a broad smile as he moved across the room towards her. 'Emma!' he exclaimed, taking her outstretched hand, and then reaching close to kiss her on the cheek. 'I'm so sorry I couldn't meet you. I wanted to very much indeed. I had planned to — '

'It's all right, Gregor,' she said, giving him a hug and a smile. 'Jennifer explained all that. How are the chicks?'

He laughed and looked embarrassed. 'Infuriating,' he said. 'I'd been monitoring that nest for weeks, and they chose today to come out. But . . . look at you! You look great.'

'It's lovely to see you again, too,' she said with another smile.

It was going to be all right, she decided. He was pleased to see her. She couldn't ask for anything more. She needn't have feared he would change his mind about seeing her again, and helping her.

'Would you like a cup of tea or coffee?' she asked. 'This is the residents' lounge. There are facilities here we can use.'

'Yes, that would be good. Thanks.'

She checked the water level in a kettle

on a little table and switched it on. 'Tea or coffee?' she asked, rummaging through a bowl of sachets and cartons.

'Coffee for me.'

She chose tea for herself, and then went through the process of emptying the sachets and teabags into cups while she waited for the kettle to boil, trying to behave as normally as she possibly could.

'What were they?' she asked over her shoulder.

'Hm?'

'The chicks.'

'Ah! The chicks. Sea eagles, actually. They're still pretty rare. So I had to stay with them.'

She nodded. 'It wasn't a problem. Jennifer met me, and we had a cup of coffee together.'

'How did you get on with her?' he asked anxiously.

'Fine. I like her. She's very nice, a lovely woman. I had met her before, you know?'

'Really? When was that?'

'The very last day on my previous visit. I was spending time in Kirkwall while I waited for the ferry. I had a look around the cathedral, and when I came out I bumped into your mother. We recognised each other and began to chat. Then Jennifer turned up, and we all went for lunch in that shop-cum-café across the road. Janet Glue's?'

Gregor nodded. 'I didn't know you'd met the rest of the family.'

'That's everybody, is it?' she asked with a smile.

'Just about!'

She finished making the tea and the coffee and set the cups down on the table. Then she sat down in a chair next to Gregor.

'It's so good to see you again,' he said. 'It really is. Oops! Have I told you that already?'

She laughed and nodded. 'But it doesn't matter. You can flatter me as much, and as often, as you like.'

They looked at each other and smiled. They were a bit stiff with each other still, but it was going to be all right, Emma thought again. She just knew it was. Somehow.

'It seems very pleasant here,' Gregor said, glancing around the room. 'It's a nice place.'

'It is. And Neil and Jenny, who run it, are lovely people. So friendly and kind.'

After a pause Gregor said, 'I've been thinking. You could do this with Broch House, if you wanted to, couldn't you?'

'What? Turn it into a guesthouse?'

He nodded.

'That possibility hadn't occurred to me, but you're right, in principle.'

'That's what Ally would do with it, if you sold it to him.'

'Oh?'

'He said so, when I saw him the other day.'

She grinned and said, 'If I did that, it might put a stop to him pestering me!'

Gregor leaned forward to pour her another cup of tea. 'It's a bit far from Newcastle, though, I suppose.'

'Isn't it?' she said softly, head on one

side, wondering what was coming next.

'You would have to give up your job.'

'That's true. I would have to have a good reason to do that, though, wouldn't I?'

Gregor paused, struggled a moment, and then changed the subject, leaving her very curious indeed about what he had been thinking. Surely he hadn't been . . . ? No, of course not. What a silly idea. All the same, she had to wonder.

'Any progress on Freda since we last spoke?' he asked briskly.

'No, nothing new to report. How about you?'

'Ah!' It was said as if he had been waiting for this moment. 'HMS Tern. You remember asking me about that ship?'

She nodded. 'Yes. What have you discovered?'

'It's not a ship at all, or it wasn't back in the day.'

'Oh?' Emma said with a frown, puzzled.

'It was a Royal Naval Station — but on land. It was a Royal Navy airfield, one of the biggest airbases in Orkney. At its peak it had nearly two thousand personnel, and getting on for a quarter of them were Wrens.'

'Really?' She leant forward, fascinated now. 'Why did they call it HMS — Her Majesty's Ship?'

'*His* Majesty's Ship!' Gregor said, grinning. 'We had a king in those days, remember? It was just what the navy did. And probably do still. Custom and tradition, I suppose. Everything seems to have been HMS, whether it was on land or water.'

'I see. So where was it, this airbase?'

'Near a village called Twatt, here in Birsay. You can still see it.'

'Oh, that's a pity,' she said, thinking of Freda and her photographs. 'So it had nothing to do with Camp Sixty?'

Gregor shook his head. 'No, nothing at all. But it is near Broch House.'

'So Freda might have had something to do with it?' she asked hopefully.

'She did, actually. Tomorrow I can take you to meet someone who says he knew Freda back then. Like her, he was stationed at HMS Tern. He's a very interesting old gentleman who my mother told me about. Would you like that?'

'I certainly would! Where does he live?'

'In Kirkwall. I haven't met him yet myself, but my mother has warned him I might call in to see him.'

'If Freda was stationed there, though,' Emma said thoughtfully, 'how could she have taken photos of Camp Sixty?'

'I don't know. Let's just see what we find out tomorrow.'

Gregor left soon afterwards. He said he had to return to the sea eagles' nest to see how the chicks were faring.

'Could I come?' Emma asked.

'Another time, perhaps. I don't want to risk frightening them by turning up in numbers. Besides, I'm likely to be there a long time tonight.'

'It's a deal. Well, thank you for all this

new information, Gregor. We're making progress at last, aren't we?'

'I think so.'

He stood up and paused rather awkwardly, as if uncertain how to tell her something else on his mind. She smiled and waited patiently.

'Emma, there is something about me you should know.'

'What's that?'

'I was married once. My wife was killed in an accident. Eight years ago.'

She could see how it was a difficult thing for him to talk about, perhaps not surprisingly.

She hastened to say, 'It's all right, Gregor. I understand, and I'm very sorry indeed. Talking about it must be very difficult. Perhaps we should do that another time, rather than now, when we're both tired after a long day. But thank you for telling me. I really do appreciate it.'

He nodded. 'Until tomorrow, then,' he said stiffly.

'Until tomorrow, Gregor.'

Afterwards, she wondered sadly how far that exchange had got them. Not very, she suspected. It seemed as if, just as Jennifer had said, Gregor was frozen in the past, unable to get out of it or speak about it. Not good.

She probably hadn't handled it very well either, she thought, feeling a bit dispirited. She should have done better. It was just that she had been so confused by the way he had spoken to her. For a moment there, when he was talking about Broch House, she had wondered what he was going to say next. *How stiff we were with one another!* she thought miserably.

Oh, well. What was done was done, and what was said was said. At least he had told her about Maggie. That was something; a shared confidence. In time, perhaps he might tell her more.

Meanwhile, she reminded herself sternly as she headed back to her room, tomorrow was another day.

27

As arranged, Emma drove into Kirkwall the next morning and met Gregor in the Tesco car park, where she was to leave her own car.

'Morning, Gregor! What a lovely day.'

He smiled and held the door of his Land Rover open for her. 'It certainly is. How are you today?'

'Wonderful, I like to think,' she replied with a grin. 'Just like the day.'

'And indeed you are. Look, we're a bit early for visiting Hamish Brown. Why don't we go back to my place for a coffee first? I live just around the corner.'

'Fine,' she said with surprise, but trying hard not to let it show. 'That sounds a good idea.'

'Let's go, then.'

Gregor's flat was upstairs in an old building that had seen better days. But the flat itself was tastefully furnished in a homely sort of way, and surprisingly tidy. At least, that was true of the living room and kitchen, the parts Emma could see.

'It's very nice,' she said with a nod of approval.

'The best part about it is the view,' Gregor advised.

She walked over to the window, from where she could see both the cathedral and the sea. 'Oh, I see what you mean. It's lovely.'

'I like watching the boats coming home to the harbour, especially at night.'

'That sounds very romantic. From my flat in Newcastle, I have a good view of the traffic on the Tyne Bridge, again especially at night, but I would quite like to see fishing boats. I suppose I ought to move to Tynemouth or North Shields.'

'Ever considered Kirkwall? Plenty of flats here.'

She nearly asked if that was an

invitation, but decided against it. She didn't want to take the risk. He might not have been amused. Instead she said, 'Not really. It's a bit too far for commuting to work.'

He laughed and urged her to sit down. 'Make yourself at home. I'm going to disappear into the kitchen and put the kettle on.'

She sat down. Almost immediately, she stood up again and began to wander, taking in the furnishings, the paintings on the wall and the contents of the bookshelves. It soon seemed to her that most of what she could see had probably not been chosen by a man. Even the books were not likely to have been selected by Gregor. Well, what had she expected?

When Gregor returned with the coffee she sat back down and smiled her thanks for the mug he handed her.

'It's got a chip in it,' he said apologetically, 'but so have all the others, I'm afraid.'

'What, this little thing? You should

see my collection of pottery. A charity shop would turn up its nose! Anyway, I like your flat, Gregor. It's very cosy. How long have you been here?'

'Ten years or so. Coming up on eleven, I think. It suits me well enough.'

'So you lived here with your wife?'

He nodded and smiled. 'It shows, does it — the feminine touch?'

'Just a bit. I didn't think the books on needlework and soft furnishings would have been your choice somehow,' she said with a grin.

'No, you're right. My stuff's in the spare bedroom. This was all set up by Maggie. It's probably time I changed things around a bit.'

Emma changed the subject. 'The gentleman we're going to visit, Gregor, this Mr Brown — you say you've never met him before?'

'No, I haven't. I only found out about him a day or two ago. I was explaining to my mother what we were trying to do, and she told me about him.'

'He won't mind us visiting him?'

'Mother said he will be thrilled. He doesn't get many visitors. Partly that's because he actually comes from one of the smaller islands, where he spent most of his life. When he could no longer manage on his own he came to Kirkwall.'

'So he won't know many people here?'

'Probably not, no. Mother knows him because she visits old folk like him, people who can't get out much anymore. Mind you, she's old folk herself now!'

'Not a bit of it! She'd a bundle of energy and fun. I enjoyed talking to her.'

'In that case, I'll get you to do it again — and give me some peace!'

★   ★   ★

Hamish Brown lived now in a modern residential home close to the Peedie Sea, a lagoon near the seafront. They were welcomed by the woman who seemed to be in charge, and assured that Mr Brown was very ready to talk to them in the main lounge. An attendant took them along to meet him.

'Some visitors for you, Hamish! More visitors, I should say.' With a wink for the benefit of Gregor and Emma, she added, 'Folk to see him are never away from the door.'

'Ha!' the elderly gentleman they had come to see remarked. 'It's a wonder they bother, Jeannie, when they see they have to get past you to do it.'

'What cheek!' Jeannie said cheerfully. 'Now, can I get you all a cup of tea, or coffee?'

After that had been sorted out, Gregor introduced Emma and himself. 'I believe my mother told you we'd like to have a chat with you, Hamish?'

'Yes, that's right, she did. Something about Freda Nicholson, in the old days, wasn't it?'

'It was, yes. Emma, here, is Freda's great-niece. She inherited Freda's house when Freda passed away, but she lives in England and doesn't know much about her. So I'm trying to help her find out a bit more. Mother told me you remember Freda when she was young, and we hoped we could to talk to you about that phase of her life.'

'I see. Yes, I remember Freda well enough. Of course I do! She became a great lady, Freda, in later life. Books, she wrote, you know?' he said, peering at Emma. 'She was on the radio and the television from time to time, as well. Talking about the islands thousands of years ago. She didn't grow up here, though. It was during the war that she first came to Orkney.'

'That's what I would like to know more about, Mr Brown,' Emma said. 'How she came here, and so on. I believe she was a Wren — with the WRNS. Did you know her in those days?'

'Yes, I did. Aye, Freda was a Wren, right enough. I was in the navy myself, but like her I didn't get to sea. We were both landlubbers!'

'Where was that, Mr Brown?'

'A place called Twatt, a navy airfield.'

'HMS Tern?'

'Yes, that's right,' he said with evident surprise. 'Have you heard of it?'

'I have, yes.'

'Well, it was a place where we looked after the navy's aircraft, you know. A big base. We were both fitters. That's what it was like in them days, men and women working together on a lot of jobs.' A twinkle came into his eye and he added, 'There were hundreds of Wrens there, like Freda. For a young man, it was a grand place to be!'

'Lucky you, Hamish!' Gregor chuckled.

'I certainly was lucky. A boy like me, from a little island like Shapinsay? I'd never seen so many young women in my life!'

Fearing the worst, Emma steered the conversation back to safer ground. 'Did Freda stay at HMS Tern throughout the war, Mr Brown?'

'Yes, I believe she did. Like me. We

233

were all there until the very end. Some were there for quite a while afterwards, as well. People weren't all demobbed at the same time, you know.'

She nodded. 'I understand. I've found some old photographs Freda took at Camp Sixty, where the Italian POWs were. But you don't think she was ever stationed there?'

The old chap gave it some thought. Something was puzzling him. Emma waited anxiously.

'Something happened,' he said slowly. 'Camp Sixty? There was . . . Oh, yes! That's it. There was an arrangement, as she called it. Freda would go to the camp sometimes because they needed her there. The commandant and the base commander at Twatt reached an understanding, I believe. Unofficially, mind.'

'Why would they need her?' Emma asked.

'To talk to them. Some of them fellows couldn't talk English.'

'The prisoners, you mean? The Italians?'

234

Hamish nodded.

'Did Freda speak Italian?'

'She did. Not just Italian either. Clever woman, Freda.'

'She must have been,' Gregor contributed. 'There won't have been many Italian speakers around in those days, not in Orkney. Apart from a few hundred Italians, that is!' he added with a grin at Emma.

'I'm amazed,' she confessed. 'But I remember my grandmother did say that Freda was good at languages.'

'She must have been,' Gregor said again.

'She was,' Hamish confirmed. 'So sometimes she would go to see the Italians. They built a chapel, you know. Just out of Nissen huts. It's still there. The Italian Chapel, they call it to this day.'

'Yes,' Emma said, nodding. 'I have Freda's photographs, and Gregor took me there. It's very interesting. Quite beautiful, as well.' With a glance at Gregor, she added, 'So we know now that Freda had a connection with Camp Sixty. There is something else I wanted to ask you, Hamish. Back then, do you know if Freda had a young man, a boyfriend, at Camp Sixty?'

'One of the Italians, you mean?'

'Yes,' she said eagerly, thinking of the photographs she had seen in Broch House.

'Oh, no!' Hamish said with a chuckle. 'That would have been fraternising with the enemy. You couldn't do that in war-time. You'd have been put up against a wall and shot.'

She let out her breath with disappointment as another theory collapsed.

'Mind you,' Hamish said, 'she did have a boyfriend. More's the pity!' he added with a chuckle.

Emma's heart rate increased again. 'Did you know him?' she asked, hardly daring to hope.

'Oh yes, I knew him quite well.'

28

'I knew him from back on Stronsay,' Hamish continued. 'I went to school with him, and everyone on the island knew everyone else anyway. I don't know so much about now, but they did then.'

'And then he came to HMS Tern, like you?'

'Well . . . not exactly. He wasn't like me in that way. I was just an aircraft fitter, a technician, like Freda. But Jamie, he was different.'

'How?' Emma prompted. 'How was he different?'

Hamish sighed and looked a little weary. Emma backed off and waited.

'More tea, Hamish?' Gregor asked gently.

'Aye, that would be good. Thank you kindly, laddie.'

Emma waited until Gregor had poured a fresh round of tea before smiling at Hamish encouragingly. 'What was Jamie like, Hamish?' she asked gently.

'Oh, he was special, was Jamie. Even as a boy he was, and even more so when he got older. He was always destined for greater things than the rest of us. That was what I always thought. He was nice enough — don't misunderstand me. Friendly and pleasant. But he had a way about him that always seemed to mean he was better than us. It made you respect him. I suppose you could say he was a natural leader. He had an air of authority about him.'

Emma let him catch his breath and be quiet for a few moments. She knew their time with him that day was coming to an end. 'Could you describe him?' she asked.

'Not a big man. Slim, average sort of build. A lot of wavy blond hair he had as a boy. I don't know about later. At Tern I only ever saw him in a flying suit and helmet.'

'He was a pilot? Air crew?' Gregor asked.

Hamish shook his head. 'A passenger.

He was always a passenger when I saw him, going out and coming in. He knew me, and we always spoke, but just a word or two. You didn't ask someone like him where he'd been or where he was going. Nothing like that. All you were told in wartime was what you needed to know. Nothing more.'

'But he and Freda hit it off?'

'They did. They were the same type of people. They were made for each other.' He paused again and sighed. 'It was just a pity that one day Jamie didn't come back. He'd been on one flight too many. Outstayed his time, as they used to say. We all knew you couldn't go on forever, doing what those fellows did. Freda was heartbroken. She wouldn't believe he wouldn't return, but he never did. That was the end of it. His time was over, and in many ways so was Freda's.'

'The Shetland Bus, maybe?' Gregor inquired gently.

'I always thought so. You couldn't ask, but I believed it was to occupied

Norway he went. Behind enemy lines.'

'So that was that,' Emma repeated quietly, saddened by Hamish's tale, if not quite sure she understood it.

'Aye, it was. She had his baby, I believe, but I never really knew anything about that. Hush-hush, it was.'

'Freda had a baby?' Emma leant forward, astonished to have confirmed what Gran had told her. 'Were they married, Freda and Jamie?'

'I don't believe they were, which was another problem in them days, but you'd have to ask my sister about that. She knows more than me.'

The old man was almost asleep by then. Emma pressed a buzzer to summon a member of staff. 'I'm afraid we've over-tired him,' she said apologetically.

'Oh, don't worry about that. When he wakes up he'll be glad you've been. Will you come again?'

'We'd like to, if it would be all right.'

'Of course it would.'

Gregor said, 'Do you know if his

sister is still alive? Hamish mentioned her, but I'm not sure if he was talking about years ago.'

'Och, yes! Moira is still with us. She's as old as Hamish nearly, but she's a very sprightly lady.'

'Is she still on Stronsay?'

'No, she's here now.'

'In Kirkwall? You don't happen to know where she lives, do you?'

'Here in this home, I meant. She's in the next wing.'

Gregor looked at Emma and said, 'We would like to see her, too, if that's possible.'

'It is, but not today. I believe she's on an outing today. Would tomorrow do?'

'Perfectly,' Emma assured her. 'Perhaps you could warn her? We'd like to talk to her about my great-aunt, Freda Nicholson. Hamish has just told us that they knew each other.'

'I'll let her know. See you tomorrow!'

29

'Well,' Emma said as they left the home, 'what did you think of that?'

'Fascinating. Come on, let's get something to eat. We can talk about it over lunch.'

Gregor knew a quiet little café tucked away in a side street near the cathedral. There were only two other people there when they arrived, an elderly couple poring over newspapers while they ate lunch.

The waitress arrived and they ordered from the daily specials menu: grilled plaice for Emma; lasagne for Gregor.

'Hamish is a charming gentleman, isn't he?' Emma suggested.

'Very much so.' Gregor smiled. 'He obviously had a shine for your great-aunt.'

'Fancy him remembering so much about her after all these years. So we got it right. Freda was in the navy, at HMS Tern — but as an aircraft technician! How weird is that?'

Gregor shrugged. 'The navy seem to have had lots of planes in those days. I'd always assumed the navy did the sailing and the RAF did the flying. Obviously it wasn't as clear-cut as that.'

'And Freda had a boyfriend?' she mused. 'That was interesting, and very sad too. But what was your comment about the Shetland Bus, or something? What was that about?'

'It was a bit of a red herring really, I suppose. But it did get Hamish to confirm what I was thinking. You see, Shetland was a jumping-off point for contact with occupied Norway during the war. Agents were sent in from there by fishing boat — spies, saboteurs, resistance fighters, and so on. Shetland was also where people like that escaped to. There was so much traffic that people called the route the Shetland Bus. They have a museum about it up there.'

'I see. But HMS Tern is, or was, on Orkney.'

'Ah, well. Agents were also parachuted into Norway, and I've no doubt some went from here.'

'So Jamie, Freda's young man, was one of those agents?'

'It's very likely. Hamish seems to think so, and I'm sure he's right. He knew the man, and working on the airfield he would have had a good idea what was going on. He knew, all right.'

'Poor Freda,' Emma murmured. 'Her man just never came back one day. That must have been awful. How do you ever get closure when something like that happens?'

Gregor grimaced. 'It must have happened a lot. Most of the people sent into France ended up the same way — in the hands of the Gestapo, and shot against a wall.'

'How terrible.'

'It makes you think how lucky we are today.'

Emma was quiet for a while. Then

she said, 'So Freda really did have a baby, just as Gran told me.'

'Yes, if Hamish remembers accurately.'

'Oh, I'm sure he does. Don't you think so?'

Gregor nodded.

'I think I would like to go back to Broch House this afternoon, to think about things. Would you come with me, Gregor?'

'Of course.' He smiled and patted her hand. 'Ah! Here's our lunch.'

*   *   *

It might be summer, Emma thought, but the house didn't feel any warmer. She shivered, earning a sympathetic grin from Gregor.

'It's so cold!' she said.

'Not really. It's just that you're not acclimatised yet.'

'You can say that again!'

The reality, of course, she thought, was that no one had been inside Broch

House since she had last shut the door. How could it be any warmer? A house needed to be lived in, by living and breathing people who switched on lights and heaters, lit fires, ran baths and opened windows when the sun was shining.

'It could soon be warmed up,' Gregor said speculatively, thinking about it. 'That is, if you wanted to have a go?'

Could it? She supposed it could. Freda had actually lived here, for goodness sake!

'Carry on yourself for a few minutes, will you?' Gregor said. 'There's one or two things outside I want to check.'

She smiled and moved on into the first of the reception rooms, and then the other one. On into the kitchen, and up to the bedrooms. All seemed to be in order. The house was just as she had left it — full of character, but still too big for one person. What on earth had Freda done here all those years?

She headed back downstairs to the storage room where Freda had kept her papers and books. That was also where the photographs were.

A few minutes later she heard Gregor calling her. 'I'm in here!' she shouted back.

'What are you doing?' he asked when he found her.

'I just had the thought that surely somewhere in here I might find a photo of Jamie. I'd like to see what he looked like.'

Gregor nodded. 'It'll take some time,' he said. 'There are an awful lot of photos.'

'Yes, and Freda didn't do a great job of organising them.'

She rummaged a few moments longer. Then, aware that Gregor was still standing in the same place, she stopped and turned to him. 'What?' she asked with a smile.

He gave her a rather sheepish grin and said, 'You know we were talking about how the house could be warmed up?'

'If someone wanted to do it?'

He nodded. 'I've just checked the yard and the shed. The oil tank is nearly full, and there's an outhouse that's well-stocked with coal and logs. How long are you here for this time?'

She stared at him for a long moment. He stared back. When he reached out to her, she saw that he no longer wore a wedding ring. She knew then that the moment she had secretly always wanted had finally arrived.

'We'll light the fire,' she said huskily, as his arms wrapped around her and he stooped to kiss her.

30

'I hope you meant that,' she said, looking up with a smile.

He hugged her close for a long moment. 'You know I did.'

'Yes,' she said happily. 'I do.'

They stayed where they were for a few more moments. Then Emma pushed him gently away. 'Come on,' she said. 'Let's light the fire.'

'Oh, we can do more than that!' Gregor said, laughing. 'Let me see if I can start the central heating system.'

'You do that, and I'll try to light a fire in the kitchen stove.'

She was in a bit of what her mother would have called a tizzy while she collected some sticks and logs for the stove in the kitchen. What was she to make of it? she wondered. What did it mean, Gregor kissing her like that? Everything, or nothing? Time would tell, she decided happily. For now, she would take one step at a time.

'Got any matches?' she called.

'No, but I've got a lighter.'

Gregor reappeared, holding out an ancient-looking zippo. He showed her how it worked.

'What about the central heating?'

'It's going — I think.'

'Clever you!'

'Nothing complicated about it. I turned the boiler on and pressed a couple of switches. Listen!'

She paused, head cocked. She could hear pipes rattling somewhere as warming water began to make its way around the house once more. 'I wonder how long it's been since that sound was last heard.'

Gregor shrugged. 'The best part of a year, I would think. Thankfully, somebody came in and turned everything off properly. So we'll keep our fingers crossed there are no burst pipes, and hope the system works like it should. How are you doing?'

She lit the newspaper she had crunched up and watched as flames spread to the thin sticks. They began to crackle immediately. Then the bigger sticks began to smoke furiously. Logs were stacked nearby, ready to go.

'I'm doing all right, I think,' Emma said, closing the stove door and turning to Gregor with a smile. 'It'll be lovely to have some heat in here.'

He nodded. 'You know what we need now, don't you?'

'What?'

'Some food. Something to cook — something to eat!'

'What a good idea,' she said, beaming at him. 'It would have to be something simple, though. I mean, I don't know how anything here works.'

'Shall I go and see what I can find?'

'Would you?' She reached out to give him a hug. 'Oh, Gregor!'

He kissed her forehead and hugged her back. 'I won't be long,' he promised.

'But where will you go? Kirkwall?'

'No, there's a little shop in the village. I'll see what they have.'

'And I'll make sure the stove doesn't go out,' she promised happily.

*   *   *

They dined on bacon and egg, artisan bread and red wine. Afterwards they made coffee.

'You managed to find everything we needed,' Emma said with approval.

'Yes. Even washing-up liquid!'

She laughed and kissed him again.

The house was scarcely any warmer, but they could feel heat from the stove now. Gregor brought more logs from the woodpile in the outhouse, and they pulled two chairs close together in front of it.

Emma felt wonderfully happy. She knew it was probably an illusion, but so what? No need to think about when the bubble burst. For now, at least, she and Gregor could be together, just as she had sometimes dreamt, but had never expected to happen.

'Happy?' Gregor asked, putting his arm around her.

She nodded and smiled, and rested her head on his shoulder. 'You?'

'Very much.'

'What's happened, Gregor?'

'Something I believe we've both wanted to happen, but perhaps felt was impossible.'

She nodded. 'You're right.'

That was all that was said just then. It seemed to be enough.

*   *   *

The afternoon turned to evening, and evening turned to night. The sun had long since disappeared beneath the horizon. Emma began to look ahead. Practical matters resumed their place on the agenda.

'So we'll see Hamish's sister in the morning?'

'Yes. That should be interesting.'

'Mm. I wonder what happened to

Jamie, and to their baby — if they really did have one.'

'Let's just wait and see what Moira has to say, shall we? No point us speculating.'

It was true. All that could wait. They didn't need to rush into the future.

After a pause, Emma said, 'Do you have your phone?'

He nodded.

'Does it work? I mean, is there coverage here?'

'Of course.'

'May I use it?'

'Yes. What for?'

'I want to call the guesthouse, to tell them I won't be back tonight.'

He looked at her quizzically, head to one side.

'I'm going to stay here.'

'You are?'

She nodded. 'There'll be somewhere to sleep, even if it's only the floor in front of the stove.'

Gregor laughed and said, 'I couldn't let you spend the night here alone.'

'No, of course you couldn't.'

'That's settled, then?'

'I think so. Don't you?'

He nodded and took her in his arms again.

31

Hamish's sister, Moira, turned out to be a very lively old lady in her late eighties. Emma could see that she suffered from arthritis, but that was only in her legs. Otherwise, she was even more together than her brother.

They met her in the residents' lounge, which was very similar to the one they had been in the previous day.

'Good morning!' she said briskly. 'You must be the two people who saw Hamish yesterday.'

'Yes, that's right. I'm Emma Mason, Freda Nicholson's niece. And this is my friend, Gregor McEwan. I believe you know Gregor's mother?'

'Yes, of course I do.' She smiled warmly at them both. 'You don't live here in Orkney, my dear?'

'No, I don't. I live in England, in Newcastle, where most of my family are.'

'Oh? I've never been, but it looks a pretty city, judging by the pictures I've seen.'

Pretty? That seemed to be stretching it a bit. Emma smiled and said, 'You must have seen pictures of the bridges over the Tyne?'

'Yes. Most impressive. We don't have such big bridges in Orkney.'

'You don't seem to need them!' Emma laughed. 'Although the Churchill Barriers are impressive enough.'

Moira smiled in acknowledgement. 'That's true. Now, how can I help you, my dear?'

'I believe you knew my great-aunt, Freda Nicholson?'

'I did, yes.'

'That's what we wanted to talk to you about. You see, I never knew her, or anything about her. But she left me her house, and I want to know more about her before I decide what to do with it.'

The old lady nodded as if she understood. 'I thought you would come one day,' she said with a faint smile.

'You did?'

Moira just nodded again. 'I'm glad to meet you at last.'

The conversation seemed to have died in its tracks, with Moira seemingly well satisfied about something, and Emma simply stunned.

'We talked to Hamish yesterday,' Gregor said quickly. 'He told us quite a bit about Freda's wartime service at Twatt. I hadn't known anything about that, although of course I knew a lot about her in more recent times.'

Moira smiled. 'Yes. Freda became quite a well-known and respected celebrity on the islands, bless her. But there won't be many of us left who knew her as a girl. It's a good thing you've come now, dear,' she added with another smile, 'while Hamish and I are both still here.'

'I'm very glad I have been able to meet you both,' Emma assured her. 'I'm glad to have learned so much about Orkney, too.'

'Already? Is this your first visit?'

She shook her head. 'I was here a couple of months ago, which was when I met Gregor and Mrs McEwan.'

'Ah! Well, you've come back at the right time now. The islands are at their best at this time of year. Where are you staying?'

'Birsay, in a guesthouse. But I've also been spending some time in Freda's house, which is nearby. Do you know it?'

'Broch House? Yes, I know it well. It'll be a bit cold and damp just now, though, I imagine.'

'Freezing!' Emma said, chuckling. 'But Gregor and I have started to warm the place up a little. We managed to get the heating going yesterday.'

'Good. It'll take a while, but I'm sure you'll soon have it cosy again.'

'It'll be a very long while before it's actually cosy, I think!'

'Emma isn't acclimatised yet,' Gregor said mischievously.

The old lady laughed, very amused, and patted Emma's hand. 'Will you live there now?' she asked. 'Freda would have liked that. I don't know, but perhaps that's what she wanted.'

'I really don't know what I'll do with the house,' Emma said hesitantly, 'but I haven't really considered living there.'

'That's a pity.'

Over coffee they chatted about everyday things. Emma was impressed by how well Moira seemed to keep up with local news and events. She was a bright lady, and clearly someone who seemed to have had quite a bit to do with Freda over the years. Emma could imagine the two of them getting on well together. No doubt Moira missed her friend greatly.

But enough of this! she eventually decided. They needed to follow up what Hamish had told them.

'Moira, Hamish told us that Freda had a boyfriend back in the days when she was stationed at Twatt during the war. From all the old photos I've found, I had started to wonder if she had a relationship with one of the Italians at

Camp Sixty. But Hamish said no, that her boyfriend was called Jamie, and that he was from the same island where you both grew up.'

'Yes, that's true. Jamie McCallan, from Stronsay.' A cloud passed across Moira's face, and she sighed. 'A lovely boy.'

'He disappeared, Hamish said,' Emma pressed. 'He didn't return from what sounded like a secret mission in Norway.'

The old lady nodded. 'Poor Jamie. He went there once too often. They all got caught, you know, in the end. You couldn't go and do that sort of thing time after time and get away with it forever. They kept him at it too long, the powers that be.'

'He just disappeared?'

'Yes. It broke Freda's heart. She waited and waited for him, but he never came back. He wasn't the only one, of course,' she added with a sad smile. 'Lots of good boys were lost in those days, one way or another. Hundreds died right here in Orkney when ships were sunk.'

It was a sombre thought. Emma waited a few moments before moving on. She took out the framed photograph, a portrait she had remembered seeing hanging on the wall in Freda's bedroom. It was of a cheerful-looking young man dressed in a fisherman's jersey. 'Is this Jamie?' she asked.

'Yes,' Moira said, glancing at the photo. 'That's him.'

Emma nodded with satisfaction. 'Hamish also told us Freda had a baby.'

'Well, he shouldn't have, the gossipy old thing!' Moira said with a chuckle. 'What's it to do with him?'

Emma smiled. 'Actually, Freda having a baby was something my grandmother mentioned one time, but she didn't say anything else about it. I didn't know whether it was true or not, to be honest. Gran's memory isn't very good now,' she added apologetically. 'I wondered if she was confused, and had got Freda mixed up with someone else. But Hamish confirmed it yesterday.' She looked at Moira expectantly.

'Well, it's true, right enough. Freda did have a baby.'

'With Jamie?'

Moira nodded. 'Yes. It was Jamie's child.'

Emma waited, wondering if there was more to come.

'The last time Freda saw Jamie, she didn't know she was pregnant,' Moira said with a sigh.

'So Jamie never knew he was a father?'

'He never knew.'

'And Freda was left a single parent?'

'For a time,' Moira said, nodding. 'That was when I came into it. But it's a long story. Are you sure you want to hear it?'

'More than ever,' Emma said firmly. 'I've waited such a long time for someone to tell me about it.'

32

'It was a lot more complicated then than it is now,' Moira said reflectively. 'For a woman in Freda's position, I mean. Unmarried mothers had a hard time in those days, quite apart from the fact that there was a war on. But I need to get things in the right order for you. First, Jamie didn't come back as expected. Freda kept going to Broch House, but there was never any news.'

'Broch House?'

'That was where Jamie, and the others like him, were based. They knew her there, you see. So she kept going, but there was never any news. In the end, they told her to keep away. They would let her know when they heard something, they said. But they never did, and she never did hear what had happened to him.'

Broch House! Emma was in a bit of a

daze, but she felt things were beginning to make sense at last.

'So Jamie didn't return,' Moira continued. 'Freda waited desperately, but there was never any news. Then she found she was pregnant. That was a calamity. Much as she might have wanted Jamie's child, pregnancy was a reason for dismissal from military service. And she didn't want to be dismissed. She wanted to wait right here for Jamie. She couldn't bear the thought of returning to England not knowing what had happened to him.'

'She did stay?'

'Yes. I'm not too sure why, or how. I don't think Freda was either. But she was important in some way, probably more because of what she did at Camp Sixty than at HMS Tern. There were lots of aircraft fitters by then, but probably not so many Italian speakers.

'So the two commanders did a deal, and kept her on as long as they could. But something else had to be done once the baby was born. There was no way

Freda could stay after that — not officially, that is. It was hard for her, but what she wanted most of all was to wait for Jamie. So it was arranged that the baby would go.'

'She gave the child up?' Emma asked, aghast.

'Reluctantly.'

'To an orphanage?'

Moira shook her head. 'No. To her sister and her husband. They had no children themselves, and they wanted a child badly. So Freda's sister came to Orkney — at a time when it was very difficult to do that — and I handed the baby over to her.'

'You?'

'It was what Freda wanted. She couldn't bear to do it herself.' Moira shrugged. 'That's how it was. That's what happened.'

'Did the baby have a name?' Emma asked, dreading the answer but needing to know.

Moira nodded. 'Yes, I remember it well. Julia, the child was called. She was a lovely little thing, and I knew that Freda's sister would take good care of her.'

Emma felt quite faint now. She was shocked beyond comprehension, able to do nothing but stare at her feet and try to control her galloping heart.

They all sat in silence for a little while. Then Emma rallied and said, 'Thank you, Moira. That's been most helpful. But I'm afraid I must go now.'

The old lady nodded with understanding. 'I'm a little tired myself, but I'm glad I've been able to tell you at last. Perhaps you could come to see me again another time?'

Emma just nodded and got up to leave, letting Gregor deal with the formalities of leaving Moira and the home itself.

Outside, in the cool, fresh air, her pulse began to slow. *I'll get used to it*, she told herself unconvincingly. More resolutely: *I must!*

Some minutes later, Gregor joined her and they walked together towards the car. 'Interesting?' he said.

'Very. Disturbing, as well,' she said with a sigh.

'Freda giving away the baby?'

'Partly that, yes.'

When they were in the car and about to move, Gregor said, 'You all right?'

She shrugged.

'Where do you want to go now?' he asked gently.

'Home,' she said. 'Broch House, I mean.'

He nodded, put the car in gear and they set off, moving along the road by the harbour, heading out past the dock where the cruise liners and the ferry to Lerwick, in Shetland, berthed.

'I think I know,' Gregor said eventually, breaking the silence that had enveloped them. 'But you'd better tell me anyway.'

She sighed and said, 'Mum's name is Julia.'

He nodded. 'And Freda's sister is your grandmother.' After a moment he added, 'No wonder you were shaken.'

'Let's just go back to Broch House, Gregor. I don't want to talk about it any more at the moment.'

33

Emma wondered if Moira was right, if her memory was true. Seventy years was a long time. Could she have got it wrong?

But whichever way she looked at it, the answer came out the same: Moira wasn't wrong. She couldn't be. She knew what had happened, all right.

Besides, Gran had told her about Freda having a baby. Immediately after that, of course, she had shut up. She must have realised too late what she was saying, and where it was likely to lead. All these years she had kept the secret!

What about Mum — Julia? Did she know? Did she know who she really was? Had the pair of them been in a life-long conspiracy to hide the truth?

How awful! So what was she to do now?

Come to terms somehow, she supposed, with the fact that Freda and Jamie were Mum's parents, and her own grandparents. Somehow she would have to find a way of doing it.

★ ★ ★

'Cup of tea?' Gregor asked quietly, holding out a steaming mug.

Emma took it gratefully. 'Thanks. Just what I needed.'

'Paracetamol as well?'

She shook her head. 'I'm not that bad,' she said, giving him a wan smile.

He joined her. They both sat staring at the flames visible through the glass panel in the front of the stove. Sipping their mugs of tea. Being together.

'In some ways,' Gregor said, 'an open fire is better, but the stove throws out the heat very nicely, and it doesn't need so much looking after.'

'I was surprised it was still alight when we came back.'

'Oh they do, these old stoves. They

can keep going for a long time.'

The routine domesticated conversation broke the tension and brought Emma back to the moment. 'I'm sorry, Gregor,' she said with a weary sigh. 'I'm not very good company at the moment, am I? It was just such a shock to learn I'm not who I've always believed I was, and that Mum isn't either. I don't know what to do about it.'

'There's no need to do anything at all, when you think about it. This situation has existed for many, many years. Nothing has really changed.'

'Perhaps not,' she admitted reluctantly. 'You know,' she added, 'I can't get over the fact that Freda gave her baby away, even if it was to her own sister.'

'A single woman with a child, waiting for her man to come home — perhaps fearing, knowing even, that he never would? How could she have coped, so far from family and friends? How would she have lived?'

Emma shook her head. 'I don't know.

It's beyond me.'

'Leave it till tomorrow,' Gregor suggested. 'We'll go back then, and talk to Moira again.'

'Yes,' she said with a yawn. 'That'll be best. At least I'm getting to know now why Freda was so estranged from the family. She must have been a true black sheep so far as they were concerned!'

'Well, maybe that's true. But perhaps she did the best she could in the circumstances.'

Emma nodded, but she wasn't convinced.

* * *

Moira seemed pleased to see them again. 'I hope you weren't too shocked by what I told you yesterday, dear?'

'It was a bit of a shock,' Emma admitted. 'You see, my mother's name is Julia.'

'I know.'

'And Gran and Grandad had only her. No other children.'

The old lady nodded as if she knew that, too. 'I had to tell you the truth. What harm can it do after all these years?'

'Does my mother know?'

'Not to my knowledge, she doesn't.'

Was that true, though? Emma thought back to Mum's evasions and prevarications. They seemed just as bad as Gran's now, and just as understandable.

'The people who brought her up are her parents, dear,' Moira said, leaning forward and speaking gently. 'There's no other way of looking at it.'

'Perhaps.'

'And there is no question at all about who your parents are, is there?'

Emma shook her head. That was certainly true. What a wise woman Moira was. She sighed and gave a wan smile. 'What I wanted to ask you, Moira, is what happened with Freda after the baby was given away. What did she do after that?'

'She waited for Jamie. She waited all her life, poor thing, although in the end even she knew he wouldn't be coming.'

'She just stayed, waiting?'

Moira nodded.

'And she bought Broch House?'

'When it came on the market many years later, she did. That was where she wanted to be while she was waiting. Nowhere else. And she didn't want anyone else either. Jamie was her man.'

It sounded desperately sad. 'And what about her baby? Did she think of her at all?'

'She did. All her life. She never forgot Julia. A woman doesn't, you know. I lost one of mine through what these days they call a cot death, but I've never forgotten him, and I've always celebrated his birthday.

'But by the time the war was over, Julia's baby had become a child, and the child was used to the only parents and home she had ever known. Freda knew it would be unforgivably selfish to tear her away. So she left things as they were — and she was the only one to suffer.'

Emma shook her head. 'She must have been a very strong person.'

'Freda? Oh, she was. Make no mistake about that.'

'Why didn't she leave her house to Mum, instead of to me?'

'She did think about it, but your parents are well settled, and quite old themselves now. So she thought it best to leave it with you. Have you seen Freda's solicitor, by the way?'

'No, not yet. I thought I should wait until I had decided what to do with the house.'

'And have you decided yet?'

'No. Why do you ask?'

'Perhaps you should see him soon. Don't wait. I believe he has something for you. A letter, I think.'

'Really? How do you know all this, Moira?'

'I was Freda's friend,' the old lady said with a gentle smile. 'She told me what she wanted you to know.'

Not much more was said after that. There didn't seem much more to say.

Soon afterwards Emma and Gregor left, having thanked Moira for what she had told them. They had reached the end of one road, but there were others still to travel.

34

There was, indeed, a letter. It was addressed to Emma, and said simply that it had been written with love, and that she — Great-aunt Freda — hoped it would be received in the same way. Broch House was hers now, to do with it as she wished. The hope was it might help Emma to enjoy an even more rich and rewarding life.

'Even now,' Emma said sadly, 'she admits nothing, does she? She maintains the fiction about her relationship to me — and it is a fiction.'

'What did you expect?' Gregor said gently. 'She was a woman who even now wouldn't want to disturb your life, or your mother's and grandmother's. It's a fine thing that she kept to the very end the promise she made to herself to hide her secret. She did the best she could. Freda was a noble woman, and a good woman. You need to remember that. She led a good life here, too. You can tell that by how well so many people speak of her.'

Emma nodded and smiled at last. 'You're so right, Gregor! At first I couldn't see it that way, but what you just said is true. Thank you for that. She stayed loyal to Jamie, too, didn't she?' she added after a moment.

'All her life. And at great cost.'

She grimaced. That was true, too.

'And what of us, Gregor? What happens to us now?'

'I can tell you what I would like to happen. But then you have a say as well.' He raised his left hand for her to see. 'Did you notice?'

'That your wedding ring has gone? Yes, I did notice. But I'm not sure what it means, Gregor.'

'Well, learning about Freda's story, which is very sad in some ways, made me reexamine my own story. When I thought about it, I knew I didn't want to continue any longer down the path Freda chose for herself. I accepted at last that I can do no more for Maggie. I need to move on. Keep the memory alive, but not live in the past — if I can. And I had come to know you, Emma,' he added with a smile. 'Now I want to travel on in my life, together with you, if that's possible.'

'Oh, Gregor! That's such a beautiful way to put it.' She paused and stared at him wonderingly. 'That's what I want, too,' she added softly.

He smiled and took her in his arms. 'I hoped you would say that,' he admitted. 'I wasn't sure, but . . . '

'Ssh!' she said. 'Just kiss me.'

★   ★   ★

Back in the family home, sharing the news about her discoveries on Orkney wasn't so fraught as Emma had anticipated. In fact, she soon lost the initiative. Mum pre-empted her.

'I expect you've worked it all out by now, have you?' she asked her with a smile.

Emma stared at her with surprise for a moment, until realisation dawned. 'You knew!' she said.

Mum nodded.

'But how — how did you know?'

'I think I've always known. I picked things up when I was a child, here and there, a bit at a time.' Mum shrugged. 'Over the years, the bits added up.'

'Well, why didn't you say something?'

'When? Who to? You, Gran?'

'Well . . . '

The answer was suddenly self-evident. There was no need to ask any more questions.

'You're just the same as Freda, Mum!' Emma said happily. 'You didn't want to upset us all, did you?'

Mum smiled. 'I had a happy life with Gran, and with Grandad when he was here. Now I have a happy life with Dad and with you. What would have been the point of putting all that at risk? Besides, Gran has looked after me all her life. I owe her so much. I wouldn't want to make her unhappy now.'

Emma shook her head and chuckled. 'Why should I be surprised? You're just the same as Freda — exactly the same!'

Dad broke in then. 'I'm glad you've got that all sorted,' he said with a big grin. 'And this is Gregor, is it?' he added, turning to greet the other visitor as he arrived at the open door.

'It is!' Emma said. 'He's just been parking the car.'

Gregor looked a little anxious as he crossed the threshold. Then he saw that all was well, and broke into a lovely smile as the introductions were made.

'Thank you,' he said, in response to the greetings. 'It's good to meet you both at last.'

'You're most welcome, lad!' Dad assured him.

And Emma knew that he truly was.

A little later, Dad asked, 'What about this house in Orkney? Have you decided yet what to do with it?'

'Broch House? Yes,' Emma assured him. 'I'm going to keep it, and we're going to run it as a guesthouse.'

'A B&B?' Mum said with surprise. 'What a lovely idea. I always wanted to do something like that myself.'

'Wouldn't have worked,' Dad said solemnly. 'Not around here, it wouldn't. But Orkney — that's different, isn't it?

'It is,' Emma assured him with delight. 'Very different. You'll love it when you come to stay with us.'

'It was my brother that gave us the idea,' Gregor added. 'He wanted to buy Broch House himself for that reason. It seemed such a good idea that we stole it from him.'

'He'll be upset about that,' Mum said anxiously. 'I hope it won't cause family problems.'

'With Alastair? No way. He'll be hunting for something else to do by now. He says he just hadn't wanted the old place falling to bits, with no one living there anymore.'

It was true, Emma thought. Alastair had been perfectly agreeable when they had told him what they were going to do.

'And Freda?' Dad asked. 'Is that all settled, as well?'

'Yes,' Emma assured him. 'She was a fine woman who led a good life in Orkney. I'm very proud of her, and I shall think of her as my other grandmother.'

She got up then and wrapped her arms around Mum, who she suspected was about to shed a tear.

'Thank you, pet!' Mum whispered. 'That was a lovely thing to say.'

Emma hugged her and glanced across at Gregor, who smiled and blew her a kiss. Everything was all right, all of it. She knew that for sure now.

We do hope that you have enjoyed reading this large print book.

Did you know that all of our titles are available for purchase?

We publish a wide range of high quality large print books including:
Romances, Mysteries, Classics
General Fiction
Non Fiction and Westerns

Special interest titles available in large print are:
The Little Oxford Dictionary
Music Book, Song Book
Hymn Book, Service Book

Also available from us courtesy of Oxford University Press:
Young Readers' Dictionary
(large print edition)
Young Readers' Thesaurus
(large print edition)

For further information or a free brochure, please contact us at:
Ulverscroft Large Print Books Ltd.,
The Green, Bradgate Road, Anstey,
Leicester, LE7 7FU, England.
Tel: (00 44) **0116 236 4325**
Fax: (00 44) **0116 234 0205**

LUCY OF LARKHILL

Christina Green

Lucy is left to run her Dartmoor farm virtually on her own after a hired hand is injured. She does her best to carry on; though when she decides to sell her baked goods direct to the public, she is forced to admit that she is overwhelmed. She needs to hire a man to help on the farm, and her childhood friend Stephen might just be the answer. But as Lucy's feelings for him grow, she is more determined than ever to remain an independent spinster . . .

FINDING HER PERFECT FAMILY

Carol MacLean

Fleeing as far as she can from an unhappy home life, Amelia Knight arrives at the tropical island of Trinita to work as a nanny at the Grenville estate. As she battles insects and tropical heat, she must also fight her increasing attraction to baby Lucio's widowed father, Leo Grenville — a man whose heart has been broken, and thus is determined never to love again. Amelia must conquer stormy weather and reveal a desperate secret before she can find her perfect family to love forever.

THE SAPPHIRE

Fay Cunningham

Cass, a talented jeweller, wants a quiet life after having helped to solve a murder case. But life is anything but dull while she lives with her mother, an eccentric witch with a penchant for attracting trouble. Now Cass's father, who left the family when she was five, is back on the scene — as well handsome detective Noel Raven, with whom Cass has an electrifying relationship. As dangers both worldly and paranormal threaten Cass and those she loves, will they be strong enough to stand together and prevail?

TROUBLE IN PARADISE

Susan Udy

When Kat's mother, Ruth, tells her that her home and shop are under threat of demolition from wealthy developer Sylvester Jordan, Kat resolves to support her struggle to stay put. So when a mysterious vandal begins to target the shop, Sylvester — or someone in his employ — is their chief suspect. However, Sylvester is also offering Kat opportunities that will support her struggling catering business — and, worst of all, she finds that the attraction she felt to him in her school days is still very much alive . . .

LAURA'S LEGACY

Valerie Holmes

Laura Pennington is the wilful daughter of self-made man Obadiah Pennington. Having risen from being a humble fisherman's daughter, she is still adjusting to her new position in society. Then fate crosses her path in the person of Mr Daniel Tranton, who catches her trespassing on private land. Together they come to the aid of a young lad who has run away from servitude at a local mill. Neither realises that the men hunting him are also set on hurting Daniel. The future depends on Laura's quick thinking and actions . . .